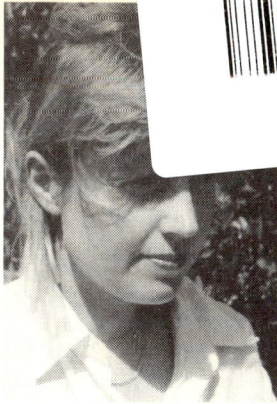

we too shall be mothers

Sallie Muirden

flamingo

An imprint of HarperCollins*Publishers*

This project has been assisted by the Commonwealth Government through the Australia Council, its arts funding and advisory body.

The author is the grateful recipient of two Australia Council Literature Board project grants which enabled her to write this book.

Flamingo

An imprint of HarperCollins*Publishers*, Australia

First published in Australia in 2001
by HarperCollins*Publishers* Pty Limited
ABN 36 009 913 517
A member of the HarperCollins*Publishers* (Australia) Pty Limited Group
http://www.harpercollins.com.au

HarperCollins*Publishers*
25 Ryde Road, Pymble, Sydney NSW 2073, Australia
31 View Road, Glenfield, Auckland 10, New Zealand
77–85 Fulham Palace Road, London W6 8JB, United Kingdom
Hazelton Lanes, 55 Avenue Road, Suite 2900, Toronto, Ontario M5R 3L2
and 1995 Markham Road, Scarborough, Ontario M1B 5M8 Canada
10 East 53rd Street, New York NY 10022, USA

National Library of Australia Cataloguing-in-Publication data:

Muirden, Sallie.
    We too shall be mothers.
    ISBN 0 7322 6692 0.
    I. Title.
A823.3

Cover design by Russell Jeffery, HarperCollins Design Studio
Cover image: *Et nous aussi nous serons mères, car ...!*, engraving, Jean-Jacques Le Queu, Paris, Bibliothèque Nationale

Printed and bound in Australia by Griffin Press on 70gsm Ensobelle

5 4 3 2 1   01 02 03 04

For Hayley and Oliver

and for Leah too

———

We have the inherent capacity
to become that which we desire.

Pico della Mirandolla

Acknowledgments

Special thanks for assistance with the editing of this novel to Antoni Jach.

Also to Louise Thurtell, Angelo Loukakis, Linda Funnell, Bronwyn Cran, Julia Stiles, Belinda Lee, Rod Morrison, Andrew Brown-May, Flora Nicoletti, Lesley Muirden and Leah Eisen.

Contents

Part 1

Contraction

I don't know how it happened,
Just now I tripped over
Onto a stone. I bruised my arm a little
And bound it with this to stop the bleeding.

The Marriage of Figaro, *Da Ponte*

1

The Convent

*T*he cloister is a real cloister. There is a locked gate, a high stone wall and a grille to sit behind when visitors come. But before God made the world, the cloister already existed in your own head. It's why you entered in the first place. It's why your head broke open when you were inside. It's why all the King's men couldn't put it back together again but the brigands who stormed the papal palace could.

After I had lived in the convent a year, I'd look at the nuns around the refectory table and see each of them with a miniature convent stuck on their wimple-bound necks. Under the veils their faces sat like cuckoo clocks with sloping chateau-style roofs.

Broken cuckoo clocks that never revealed their birds. Tight mouths. Tight wimples. Convent faces with sealed windows and indented smiles.

When I entered the convent we novices had to perform a symbolic key-throwing ceremony. It was a kind of initiation into the life of the veil. We'd go into the garden and fling a key over one of the walls, into the sacristy orchard, as far as we could throw. We were given keys that no-one wanted. Old keys that opened no doors, or none that could be found or remembered. We were throwing away our attachment to the old world. To our families. To matrimony and motherhood. (Some of us were throwing away our dreams.)

When I threw my key over the wall, someone on the other side (perhaps a gardener working there) threw it straight back. It landed at my feet. The nuns all looked at me. There was an omen in this, the Reverend Mother said.

'Shall I try again?' The nuns shook their heads and our company moved slowly back indoors, out of the sunlight.

Years later, when my mind broke into pieces and I was trying to put it back together, I tried all the locks in the convent with the initiation key I'd kept in a drawer alongside my narrow bed. The nuns let me go from door to door like a janitor, rattling my key in one keyhole after another. Ruining some of the locks. They humoured me for they could see I wasn't myself.

'The key doesn't open any of the doors in the convent,' the Reverend Mother said, sitting me down and patting the palm of my hand.

'The key doesn't open any of the doors,' I repeated, trying to convince myself of the fact.

I still believed I was looking for a way in, when in fact I was looking for a way out. 'I'm not a good enough nun,' I lamented.

'Strive to be better,' the Reverend Mother encouraged. I strove, broken crown and all. In Paris the sans-cullottes were striving too. They pulled down an old fortress in a matter of days.

You'd expect our Carmelite motto to be *Strive to be better*, as this was what we were told nearly every day of the week. It wasn't. Our Carmelite motto was *Know thyself*, which was an odd one because none of us knew anything about ourselves.

We knew everything about the Holy Family and most of what there was to know about God, which wasn't much at all, but we knew nothing about ourselves.

With my broken head (that which exists only two hand spans above a broken heart) I could say the things that needed to be said. I could say I needed someone to love. I could say I wanted a child.

I had no reason but I made great sense.

The nuns laughed awkwardly. They didn't want me to have these things even if they'd never wanted them for themselves. They wanted to keep me in the cloister; another young face among the old, singing the Miserere on Sundays as we congregated behind the church organ where we could be heard but not seen.

I was the convent jester with a brown paper crown on my head. I chattered away to myself or to anyone who would listen. Too sick to hear my own words. Too honest to be taken seriously.

Distracted by the northern Parisian strife our Reverend Mother took pity on me and released me from my vows. Our King was dead, our Queen still languishing in gaol. The sisters had finally agreed to take the oath of liberty and equality, but in defiance of the new constitutional laws they still wore religious habits. And none of them chose to leave the convent, even when Saint Catherine's was pillaged by revolutionary guards and the atrocities against priests began.

Before God made the world the cloister existed in their own heads. (The sisters continued to say mass with a chaplain hidden under the refectory floorboards.)

The day my family came to collect me the Reverend Mother told me to make a good marriage and put aside my foolish romantic dreams. She told me that if I had a child I would find happiness in that child.

The Reverend Mother had never spoken of such worldly things to me before. She obviously had one gospel for those in the cloister and another for those outside.

'Are you saying don't marry for love?' I asked.

'Do nothing without love! But don't fall in love unless you can help it.'

I wondered how you could do one without the other. It was that word *love* again, with its confusing variety of meanings. What could she know of menfolk and babies, this fifty-year-old virgin? I smiled forgivingly at her and one innocent clasped the hand of another in farewell.

It was spring, 1793. I returned with Mama to our family home in the Rue Joseph Vernet with the well-pruned maple trees lining the street. Honeycomb dwellings stretched this way and that, as far as the eye could see. (Oh how I had missed you, Avignon, with your purple vines and gold orange groves.)

Mama got out my old dresses from the cedar trunk in the attic and I tried them on. Years of fasting and regular meals had kept me slim. I was twenty-seven but closer to twenty in spirit, with a huge overloaded conscience I took off like a nail-studded bonnet and put away in the chest along with my nun's habit and veil and a bundle of leftover sleep.

My little brothers were all bigger than me now. As I cuddled my tiny newborn niece, I could feel my heart shrinking back to its former size. Mama and Papa were relieved to have me home. During the day it was quiet in the house with my brothers living or working elsewhere. My mother said it reminded her of my first years when there were just the three of us. She'd gaze at me fondly and I'd know she was thinking of me as an infant. She'd told me I was the one great love of her life. The 'little me' that is. The 'big me' she found rather more of a trial.

To escape her cloying presence I crossed the road and helped my father in his music shop. I repaired a harp under his instruction. When I began mending the harp it was like an open window. Securing the strings was hard work and my fingers cracked and bled.

Gradually they toughened up. There was a sense of achievement with the instrument completed.

In my father's presence (when there were just the two of us) I always felt an emptiness which I knew to be my mother's absence. I think Papa felt it too.

'Should you love with your heart or with your body,' I asked my father when I was seven years old. (The boy across the road had refused to play with me because I was a girl. It was my body which was at fault in this instance, I supposed.)

'Your heart is part of your body,' was all my papa would say, and he picked me up by my heels and swung me around and around as though to prove the point.

I asked my mother the same question but her answer was different.

'Given the absence of both things, you should always love with your heart. Never with your body alone.'

I nodded, pretending to be worldly-wise. I understood the logic of her words. I loved to ask my parents huge questions and watch them stagger under the weight, digesting them then coming up with suitable answers for a child who was ageing faster than her slowly turning years.

I had no desire to grow up quickly. I wanted to know everything immediately and rule the world as a child. The small hermit child holds her heart inside the cave of her body. There is no question of severance between the two here. Her body belongs to her mother, father and brothers. Her heart makes intimate communion with the world every day through these physical images that are as bread and milk to her lips. Mother, brother, father. One body folds into another. The fantasy of the union which created her makes her own loving possible now and in the distant future.

'Mama, the boy across the road doesn't love me any more because my body is a girl's.'

'Marie-France, the boy across the road has no sisters. That can be a problem sometimes.'

In the convent where we had no brothers of any kind (only our chaplain who was an uncle of sorts), we loved with our hearts and not our bodies. There was always a good reason for doing so and we had found many in our lives before incarceration. We arrived with our pockets full of keys that had failed to open doors in the outside world. These keys were pockmarked with small indentations (from probing into locks they could never turn) and some were inscribed with the place names of fictional towns where beautiful people lived and reigned.

I had once unlocked the door of a fictional town but all the people there were too old and too tall for me. They wore their crowns rolled up their sleeves and patted me on the head as I ducked beneath their branches and leaves. Click went my key in the lock of a second town but this time everyone was smaller than me. Very fair, very wise, but they were all under seven and their broad crowns rested like ruffs round their necks. I walked among them like an old, old seer. Everything is relative and I was fourteen. Fertility ages girls so fast that upon the first sight of blood some find grey hairs sprouting among the black.

In my nightmare Mama was drowning in a well. I was trying to bucket the water out, to save her. I could see her face disappearing at the end of the tunnel, her mouth pouting upwards like the mouth of a fish. She was looking at me in despair. I had to get the water out quickly. I panicked. I pulled the bucket up too hastily and its contents spilled down upon her, finishing her off. Down she sank, down, down, and out of sight.

It was my mother's body I was wanting. As a child, in the convent, even now as I'm writing this. Her body had given me life but it had also let me down. Dwindling breast milk was the start of my overattachment.

My father had never let me down. His was the one magnanimous love. No man could betray me because my father never had.

(When you finally let go you can find yourself again in the wellspring of others.)

In the vestibule of our convent a large basket was overflowing with forsaken keys. Small instruments of personal defeat. In the lone hour of sunshine which pierced through the stone walls, the basket shone like a cradle full of hook-eye fish.

Yet it would not be true to say we entered to avoid life. For some of us it was our way into life through the back door of our minds. I found that out. You can close the front door but the back door remains open, and when you're sleeping any animal in the forest can walk into your room and lie down beside you.

Our hearts overruled our bodies but at times our blood could not be restrained. Pregnancy was our way of expressing desire.

'I'm pregnant for you,' Sister Catherine said to me, stroking an imaginary child in her womb.

'Is it my child?' I asked, touching her womb through the rough hemp of her habit. She was naked beneath for we weren't allowed the luxury of underclothes.

We did no more than ever flirt with the suggestive folds of our rook-black gowns, wondering about the unexplored worlds beneath. Each of us harboured an absurd desire to curl up beneath the divinity of the Reverend Mother's habit (how much fuller and softer than our own gowns it seemed) and crouching there to reach out through the curtain of her skirts for that girdle hanging down from her waist. Then to chew on its knots like hungry sheep.

Spurred on by their desire for love, some sisters stitched Babylonian red quilts which newlyweds would romp beneath or whole families muster under on winter nights. In the time it took to make one quilt, fields of local children were conceived, born and raised toward maturity.

The convent was a resting house between waking and living. Being inside wasn't like dying. Not really. It was more of a lying-in. Mother Thérèse had a few madcap ideas up her sleeve which went against the prevailing Carmelite doctrine. We were allowed to touch each other as we practised laying out the dead. '*Veni Creator*,' the Reverend Mother sang. Oh, it was a great game, the only times we saw each other naked except when we washed our chicken skins with tar soap in the freezing cold tub.

I'd pretend I was dead, I'd lie there in a state of rigor mortis (more from cold than any pronounced acting ability) with Mother Thérèse presiding, crossing herself rhythmically like a conductor directing her musicians.

Catherine would rub me all over with pieces of fresh lemon as if I was a fish about to be baked in a shallow dish. There was nothing sensual about this basting because the whole process was designed to eliminate my body's natural odours and excretions. A sponge soaked in vinegar dampened any chance of arousal and Catherine's fingers never brushed my skin, even by accident. Mother Thérèse was watching me anyway, watching my every movement in case I upset the illusion of mortality.

Yet I *was* being touched. I was being cared for in the only way I could imagine possible.

Did my soul depart my body on these occasions? I don't know. I felt sometimes my soul was a small ball being tossed to and fro by Thérèse and Catherine. Back and forth I went, like a ball in a children's game. My little tufted cloud of soul. Were they protecting it for me or keeping it from me?

My spirit was another matter. Oh, my spirit! I have no doubt it departed my body at the very moment I lay down and submitted to this travesty of lovemaking, this dousing of desire. Each nun was determined to prove herself more repressed than any other and no-one more so than myself.

My spirit would always listen for a sound outside the convent (hoof-trots, a jingle of a bridle, the outraged shout of someone pickpocketed) and cling to that so it was no longer in Thérèse's parlour keeping me company on the nail-studded bed. My spirit escaped and was dancing down the street, leaping from carriage to carriage, from roof to treetop like a forest fire chasing the waving fringes of the trees.

But my soul was made from a vaporous substance and would never depart my body unless I was truly dead. Small tufts could be pulled free and acted upon by others, like the white ball thrown by Thérèse and Catherine, but my soul felt for my body what a vampire feels for his blood: a total mystification and dependency.

After Sister Catherine had purified my body the orifices needed to be symbolically closed. The basket of forsaken keys was brought into Thérèse's parlour and Catherine pulled a bunch from its inner reaches. I opened my mouth expectantly. Catherine put the end of a key in my mouth and I chomped on it. A bit going into a horse's mouth. Catherine laughed. She turned the key in its lock and as she withdrew it I sealed my lips as though for the last time.

Then I spread my legs for her. She nestled the key against my sex. She did not push it inside. Her nature was too delicate for that. Besides, it was against our teaching. She pressed its coldness against me and I reacted as I was supposed to. I felt my body grow as hard and impenetrable as a diamond. Catherine said a prayer and withdrew the key.

And then we felt it, all three of us. A wave of sadness and lament and loss that we had been born virgins and were going to die virgins. Our bodies had been made for love but we weren't going to be the ones to receive any. Not even once in a corn-throbbing field, nor in a blind alley furtively, nor amongst the bulrushes of our river before and after marriage.

I never felt that way about my barrenness. I was too young to have regret on that score. The older women said they did. Some of them. But my virginity was always on my mind, for that part of me Catherine's key rested against never ceased to ache expectantly as though it was forever waiting to be filled.

How did we come to live like that?

History was against us and our country of birth perhaps, but I remember that grey patch ingrained in each sister's face, a greyness I did not see in the faces of women outside the convent. When the sisters held their candles out before them on our processional to bed, you could see those patches most clearly. They predated confinement. Forget about haloes and holy wings encircling our veils.

A grey patch the shape of a bruise, the size of a peach. An identifying mark of our own making.

There was something in nearly all of us which preferred sleep to life.

In the convent our hearts grew too big for our bodies. The unnatural circumstances we were subjected to caused an enlarged growth in that place where feelings are supposed to collect, like tributaries running back to their source.

I had felt my heart growing from my first days in the convent. When we went to bed I would lie on my back feeling an abnormal pressure against my ribs. The noise inside my chest was alarming.

'My heart is beating too loudly,' I told Mother Thérèse, ashamed and frightened at the same time.

'Oh that's what happens. It'll only get louder. It's God's presence inside you. God's heartbeat.'

I was so worried I asked our convent doctor to examine me.

'Is God beating in my breast?'

'No, your heart is increasing in size. Every second or third nun suffers from the same complaint.'

'What causes it?'

'Not enough love on the outside makes the heart compensate on the inside,' the doctor said matter-of-factly.

I nodded. Already I had experienced that burning love sensation which seemed to come from nowhere but within me. Jesus was love and Mary was love and loving was what we might do with unrestricted abandon in this shadow land where marriage to God protected us from every harm. Not a company of bleeding hearts, but a company of beating hearts! And so we were. Our bodies wasted away but the swelling red organ inside rallied on.

Heart attacks between the ages of forty and fifty usually killed us, Doctor Thoreau told me. Huge hearts the size of human brains or stallions' hearts he had sometimes removed from the bodies of dead sisters and squeezed into pickle jars to be peered at by medical students in faraway Paris.

In the chapel, in the refectory, we were deafened by

the music of love. It was a noisy love. A dependable love. A symphonic love. We had to hang bells round the necks of the older sisters to drown out their deafening drum rolls. It was like living back inside the womb and listening to the giant mother heartbeat. When the entire company met for meals we had to raise our voices to hear each other speak.

Sitting in the chapel our prayers needed to be chanted in time with the rhythm of our inner clocks. Our chaplain was forced to conduct us musically with his crucifix as he performed the liturgy. It was something he had grown accustomed to, but still deeply resented.

I got used to the sound of blood pumping through my arteries. I got used to the barrage of my heart proclaiming its mystery (and mastery) of love.

The ones with the heartbeats became my friends because they were the most like me. There was no question about opening up to others. We were the sisters who wore our hearts on our sleeve.

There was an ageing sister who had asked Doctor Thoreau, in desperation, to pierce her eardrums, but that was a rare case.

At odd times I loved the noise. It gave me joy even though I knew one day my heart would burst. And it would get louder and louder. Oh ecstasy of Saint Teresa! Louder and louder. All heart I would be, with my body swinging from it like wet clothes from a peg. Hanging on for dear life.

When Sister Genevieve died there was nothing vaguely religious or gratifying about it. And when we came to lay her out I found grey skin all over her shrunken body. Her left breast was a mountain towering over her right. Inside that mountain her giant heart had been sheltering all those years. Oceans of blood had safely coursed through her, circling and circling, endlessly searching, looking for a way out and not finding one.

No-one could say her heart hadn't lived, but that skin told its own story. Undeniably her body had not.

2

Giselle's Mistake

As small girls Giselle and I used to play at being nuns.

In my attic room we would drop down veils (tied together in knots) to boys who passed by on donkeys, or after school, hugging their books against their chests. When they tugged on these twisting veils (with curiosity or in annoyance) we would pull them up quickly and close the shutters forcefully. If the boys threw pebbles at our shutters we would open them a little and smile provocatively, but we wouldn't lower our veils to them again.

One of these boys, a friend of my brother Julian, was so irritated by our little game he decided to punish us with a little game-playing of his own. When we closed the shutters on him he disappeared down the laneway and invited himself into our house through the back door on pretence of visiting Julian. He was up the stairs in leaps and bounds and at the attic door confronting us, the gleeful expression dying on his face as he wondered what on earth he was going to say.

We looked at him, he looked at us. Giselle and I did not want to play with him or talk to him. He did not really want to play with or talk to us. After a few uncomfortable seconds he ran away to find my brother. Giselle and I went back to playing nuns.

We would bind each other's necks and heads in the satin sashes from our communion dresses. These pink wimples shimmering beneath our black veils made us look like girls from a sultan's harem, and as we often wore jewellery (an offence in a real convent) we looked like we belonged to some wild caste of child nuns.

We stole sheets from my mother's linen cupboard and curtains from the downstairs parlour and joined them together with gold clasps. The linen was finely twined and the curtains made of purple, red and crimson stuffs. We fastened the sheets to the attic rafters and made a tent to lie inside. Naked from neck to toe, smooth linen fell on us from above and a luxurious softness brushed against our buttocks and thighs from the sheepskin rugs beneath.

Under the canopy of caressing curtains and sheets, Giselle stood up and I closed my eyes. She opened a bag of swans' down and tipped it over me. (Then I did the same to her.) We licked orange blossoms and stuck them to each other's skin making swirling patterns that resembled the contours of countries we wanted to go to in our dreams. Off to Turkey and Egypt we went.

Our bodies were just beginning to know themselves. The feelings existing in that cavity between our ribcages (those we had long since known about) were connected to a new and very persuasive meeting place residing between our legs (speak up, you orators, speak up!).

Giselle and I would take pleasure in calling ourselves *Sister* for neither of us had sisters in the true sense of the word. I had younger brothers and my best friend was an only child. Sometimes we'd let the boys enter our tent if we were properly dressed. Then it would only be a matter of time before the walls fell in after frantic tugging on loops and clasps.

If we wanted to escape my brothers altogether we'd take to the streets in our gipsy-nun outfits. We'd follow the trail of Ursulines as they took their afternoon stroll along the avenues of Avignon. We'd traipse at the tail of their neat black column, a foot shorter than the women in front. We were an odd-looking addition to the line for our combination habits had been adorned with other items from my dress-up chest. Giselle would wear a pair of high-heeled dancing shoes which made a furious clatter across the cobblestones as we pursued and mimicked the older women. A flock of petticoats filled out the sacks of our habits so that we were forever chasing our skirts as they flirted with a choreographical, enveloping wind.

The Ursuline sisters (who were going to teach us devotions and etiquette in a few years time) would look around at us benevolently and sometimes smile, but their walking pace was formidable and we had to half run to keep up with them. Giselle's flowing veil would get caught under the heels of her shoes and be torn and ragged by the time we ambled our way home.

Inevitably we ended up on the Bridge of Avignon where the Ursuline company halted. Here the nuns drew in deep breaths and looked up at the sky as though they were looking directly into the eyes of God. Giselle and I copied them as best we could panting and bending over, for the trot up the hill had usually given us stitches in our sides. We followed the direction of the nuns' eyes, salvaging the sky for a holy sign or star. An upside-down sea drained of colour and movement. A grey sky was never inspiring to me.

'I think I can see it,' said Giselle expectantly.

'What? What?' (How many times can you say 'what' without sounding like a fool?) 'Oh there. Oh, oh. But what is it?'

Giselle thought she knew. Perhaps she did. She crossed herself at the same time as the sisters.

'Au revoir, little girls.' The Reverend Mother brushed past us, taking her column of nuns back down the hill with her.

We were usually too tired to follow them and I was still wondering about the secrets the sky was withholding from my gaze. Giselle and I watched the disappearing caterpillar of nuns. Windblown, we would climb down from the parapet and make a beeline for the cathedral which we regarded as our own special convent. This monumental edifice had no order of nuns attached to it so we liked to think of it as ours and ours alone.

Giselle and I would walk around in the darkness, genuflecting and praying in one brilliantly lit side-chapel after another. (Praying at the age of nine meant closing our eyes and humming a tune.) We would blow out a row of candles then light them again, blow them out then light them again.

I felt myself a real nun at these moments when we trespassed across the hexagonal tiles, hugging the statue of Saint Anne as though she was our own mother. Playing hide-and-seek among the pillars of stone. As a child of nine I felt more of a nun than I ever felt myself to be when I entered a real convent eight years later. In my time with the Carmelites I was always trying to recapture those days as girls modelling ourselves on the Ursulines whose lives were the figments of our fertile imaginations.

I was always waiting for that special moment when I would feel exactly as I had when Giselle and I stood in the nave in a fountain of stained-glass light and held up our arms to capture the streaming rays. The rest of the cathedral was darkness but upon this one stone, directly in front of the altar, the light from twelve amber windows converged in a star of glowing centripetal warmth.

Whichever way Giselle and I turned, the light caught us in its golden beams. We raised our arms and caught those beams in our cupped hands. Chalices, golden chalices, we received into our hands, and when we dropped our arms, the chalices spilt their brilliant contents down upon us, drenching us with a warmth that bathed rather than burned. The light cascaded off our bodies and splashed onto our feet and the stone tiles upon which we stood.

We knelt down and touched the huge hexagonal stone with our palms. It was hot. As hot as the surrounds of a fireplace when the fire is alive. (Yet all the other tiles in the cathedral were stone-cold.) We touched our shoes which were feverishly hot too, though the feet inside them were no warmer than the rest of our bodies.

Giselle jumped off the burning tile and the rays no longer caught her in their honeyed embrace. I wanted to stay inside the star of warmth but I didn't want to do so without my friend. I could have stayed within that light forever, been transformed into golden particles and not minded.

But I wanted Giselle more than I wanted the light so I hopped off the tile, following her fleet-footed retreat, and again I was at the mercy of cold dark surrounds and the shadowy portals contained within the mighty walls. The warmth still radiated through me and when I looked at Giselle she had a golden aura around her body. I couldn't see any dust motes on myself but Giselle could for she began brushing me down as though I was covered in hay. The colour slowly faded from her body. She grabbed my hand and pulled me towards the chapel of Saint Anne. Her forehead was lined with worry.

In the privacy of the chapel she took off her boot and showed me a small hole burnt through the toe. It must have been the shower of God burning her boot like sunlight through a magnifying glass. Giselle's woollen stocking had a singed look in the region of the toe, though there was no actual hole in the stocking itself. Giselle gave me her 'we've-done-something-wrong' look and I responded with my 'don't-be-so-silly-that-was-great-fun' shrug.

Giselle didn't need that amber warmth as much as I did. She had it in her own home from her parents and her grandparents and from her fruit-growing relatives living in the neighbouring countryside. I didn't have that warmth in my family. There was love, an essentially restrained love, but not that convivial warmth I felt when I was staying at Giselle's house where orchard people were always laughing and cracking jokes and making hot drinks for one another. And I had the unruliness of my brothers to deal with on a daily basis for I was partly responsible for raising them. Their rough play was draining on my nerves and when they turned on me it would take all my strength to fend them off. Bruises were the rule of the day.

I needed that golden fountain of love, and when I was seventeen and Giselle died I needed it more than ever. Entering the convent I naively believed I would find it again with the other novices. I would rediscover what I had known with Giselle.

But living in a convent there was nothing to imagine about being a nun any more. Indeed there was much to resent about a place that fell so far short of my ideal of what a convent was supposed to be. When I began to dream of the outside world a year after taking my vows, I knew the convent had failed me but I still believed I owed it my life. I was determined not to fail the convent. It wasn't because of my vows. It wasn't a question of pride. It wasn't even about my loyalty to the other women.

In the convent I could dream to excess and the cold light of day could never shatter these profound longings. I did not believe my inner world could be of value to anyone else. Certainly not to God. Ashamed of its existence, I was determined to preserve it for my sole enjoyment as long as I could.

The sisters would kneel before the altar and reel off prayers, fingers twisting at rosaries, and I would close my eyes and imagine myself in another world, in medieval Flanders skating across a river of smoking ice, landing headfirst in an Easter garden of Dutch irises. While we sat for hours making the gilt-edged *paperoles* for our benefactors, my mind was free to come and go as it pleased. As I curled the strips of paper with as much care as young girls curl each other's fringes, I was lying on nearby Lure Mountain, a lover draping my naked body in purple wisteria as almond blossom fell on us like snow.

The convent was my benefactor. I owed it everything. The gospel of each day confirmed my belief that love could never be fulfilled in the outside world. (Believe only in God's miracles, we were told.) The sermon of the day which we had heard so many times before was a clear invitation to find a private means of satisfying oneself. We all have our little ways of surviving and mine were the only ones I knew.

If I had told the Reverend Mother that once, in a cathedral, I had drowned in a warm fountain of God's love, she would have cautioned me not to grow drunk on my own dreams. Were I to ask if the hole in Giselle's boot constituted a miracle, she would have said that miracles were only performed for the benefit of others and what good had that hole in Giselle's boot done for anyone else?

In the cathedral, when it happened, Giselle and I thought the hole meant we'd either done something very good or very bad. We weren't sure which. My friend was still frowning when we saw a young priest appear, for the hour of mass was almost upon us. When it became apparent he had seen us and was moving in our direction, Giselle squatted down behind my puffed-out skirt and hid there while he was talking to me. Of course he had already seen her. He knew she was there.

The priest made the sign of the cross over us. 'Good little girls. You will be sisters one day?' He was considering with amusement the veil trailing behind me and the garish pink wimple encircling my face.

'No, Father, we want to be mothers.'

He smiled as though this was also a pleasant thought.

'Here's a candle to light and one for your friend. Pray for all the mothers-to-be.' Then he strode away, disappearing through a door behind the choir stalls. We scuttled out into the daylight, taking the candles with us. They were beeswax candles inscribed with Latin proverbs. We would keep them in a safe place (in Giselle's house away from my pillaging brothers) and bring them out again for midnight mass.

What I told the priest about us wanting to be mothers was true. We played at being nuns but we did not intend to take the veil ourselves. Not if we had any say in the matter we wouldn't. We knew you couldn't be both a mother and a nun, but we did not know exactly why. Only at rare times, when I saw my mother standing behind a religious sister waiting to enter the confessional, did I wonder about this.

What was it the mother possessed which the nun didn't? What did the nun know about God which the mother could never aspire to know? When did one know one was meant to be a mother? When could one be sure that one was truly a nun and that the religious vocation was the right choice?

We knew our mothers could never become nuns. There was something about a mother's body that made this conversion impossible, or extremely unlikely. But could a nun become a mother? Could she leave her convent and start again? Occasionally you heard of a novice who didn't go on to take her final vows. What if one made a mistake? Giselle made a mistake, though perhaps that was never obvious to her.

Giselle and I both wanted to have children when we grew up, and whilst we were children we wanted to play romantically at being nuns. Giselle wanted to have one child and I wanted a dozen. These much-insisted-upon figures met with mild reproval from our mothers. One child was far too few, Giselle's mama said. And twelve was half a dozen too many, objected my own hard-working mother.

Giselle wanted to replicate herself, that's what I think. She was an only child and she wanted to produce another only child. She was sure it would be a girl. I was excessive, even greedy in my imagination. Although twelve children was an improbable number for one woman to bear, I would arrive at the figure by a process of multiple births. Three lots of twins and two lots of triplets would get me to my goal in no time. Five confinements was surely enough. One shouldn't tempt fate. My own mother had stopped at five, though she claimed only ill-health made her do so. Mama encouraged me to consider the practicalities of feeding such a bountiful brood but I didn't spare a thought for that. Giselle and I knew we couldn't live without children. As far as men were concerned, they weren't in the picture for us yet.

Although we both wanted to be mothers, as young girls we never played with dolls. My younger brothers, as babies, had fulfilled the function of dolls in my life. The youngest one, Emile, a two year old, was still a doll of sorts. He liked to be picked up and fondled. He was always following Giselle and me around as if we were his single mother split into two. Giselle had a doll that sat on her bed but she never played with it. She'd throw it at me from time to time when she was angry with me. Mostly her temperament was placid but occasionally she stoked up like a fire and attacked me.

We had become friends at the ages of seven and eight when we already understood a lot of our likes and dislikes about ourselves and others. We became friends by choice, yet chance had thrown us together and fate was to separate us well before our diverging natures would have done so of their own accord.

I loved her yes, but I never recognised it as love. I didn't even think of her as my special friend, yet she was part of my week, my thoughts, my life. I gravitated to her side, I spent all my free time with her. She said she felt proud to be my friend walking along the streets of Avignon, but I never considered my feelings for her in this way. She was the lover and I was the beloved, if you can use such terms to describe the closeness between girls. It was like that six days out of seven until she met Philippe. On the seventh day (and after she'd met Philippe) I became the lover and she was my beloved.

As the beloved I depended upon a constant manifestation of Giselle's love for me, while remaining ignorant of my own depth of reciprocal feeling. Perhaps an unconscious part of me knew the strength of the bond, for as we grew older I sometimes longed for our friendship to be over. Each year added a weight to the scales upon which our unity balanced and these weights threatened my desire to grow free of human entanglements.

At fourteen and fifteen (Giselle was the older) we were still as close as a pair of shackled ponies but our friendship had altered and we no longer played at being nuns. Instead Giselle spent hours embroidering cashmere shawls to wear over her floral blouses and the red and white striped market-day skirts that suited her so well. With her beaming smile and her inner confidence she was the most attractive girl to be seen carrying a basket in our town square, apart from the Jewish girls with their distinctive yellow ribbons, who were the undisputed beauties of our town. Giselle, head bent down and a thimble on her forefinger, would sew as we walked to and from the Ursuline convent. I would read a book and she would sew. We both stumbled and knocked into things. People cried, 'Look out!', often when it was too late.

Characters in the books I was reading began to take the place of my friend in my affections. My wealthy aunt in Paris sent me copies of the very popular Diderot's *Les Baisers* and Voltaire's *Princesse de Babylone*, but the editions I read from cover to cover were the *romans de femmes* which told the stories of real people in the letters and histories of our time. Mme de Villeneuve, Mlle de Milly, Mme Benoist, Mme Riccononi, Mme de Monbart and Mlle Motte — theirs were the books I read along the road while Giselle sewed, hair falling down over her eyes, stopping to bite at the ends of her thread and sometimes to squint at the overhead sun. Always when the stories were made up I wanted to know if the fictional characters were modelled on real people. I badgered my aunt to find out the facts from her salon-frequenting friends, and these stories about the stories kept me entertained when Giselle went missing and I had barely begun to notice her gone.

We hadn't run out of things to say to each other. But we had run out of the thread of childhood which had held us so protectively in its web for seven contented years. (Giselle had run out of thread. Strictly speaking I had not.) My friend was waiting patiently for me to catch on to the changes which were swirling her on in life ahead of me. She led the way, hoping I would follow, sooner or later. She certainly wasn't going to drag me after her. That wasn't her style. I noted her example, I remarked upon it many times, but copy her I refused to do.

Giselle was picking up sophisticated womanly charms, like swinging her body from the hips as she walked, rather than letting her knees carry her weight as they'd done in the past. I'd notice these changes and feel resentful. 'Are you walking like that for any particular reason?' I'd ask.

I should have copied Giselle like the other young women were doing. (And she would have been more than happy for me to do so.) I shunned the face of the crowd at the market fair, wearing a communion gown I had long since outgrown. I refused to curl my hair and I lied about my age.

My harpsichord became my needle and thread, and while Giselle sewed her wedding trousseau sitting on the sofa in our parlour I stitched my fingers to the keyboard, playing minuets and bourrées as though the notes themselves were the only friends I could trust. While she sat on the sofa and embroidered a future for herself, inscribing silk and taffeta with her own symbols (white carnation and bryony rose), I sat at the harpsichord and fastened my fingers to the ivory assurances of the past. The composers of these traditional tunes had surely written their music to soothe others. Perhaps they also wanted to save their feelings from the belligerence of the world.

I practised my scales fanatically so that my technique improved, but the music itself was a monotonous stream without shade or colour. My music-teaching father would come into the parlour saying, 'A Boccherini minuet makes a strange funeral march,' and my violinist cousin Emmanuel would stick his head round the door and say, 'I'm going to make you cry, Marie-France, just to make you play better. Sorry, but I'm going to have to make you cry.'

Giselle did not care for music and I did not care for sewing. Though we still spent our days together, a new formality had sprung up between us. At the age of fifteen, having painstakingly laboured over her trousseau of wedding clothes, Giselle began to wear them in preparation for the future. She said she was getting herself in the mood for marriage. She wore a white *boutis* petticoat covered by an ottoman dress and over this a muslin shawl fastened with four silver pins. And to the band around her waist she secured a ring from which she said she would hang the key to her postnuptial home.

She wore her wedding clothes obsessively, anticipating all that was to come as though she was actually experiencing it in the present. She put on her silk-spun clothes each day before and after school. She wore them to mass where people thought she was trying to draw attention to herself or had undergone a religious conversion of some kind. 'Saint or sinner,' they muttered under their breath. They weren't sure which.

I knew she was neither.

Although she had no husband to marry this made no difference to my friend. Husband or no husband she was ready to leave home right now. She needed no flesh-and-blood suitor to grab hold of, so consumed was she by the fires of her own beautiful conflagration.

The knowledge of a passionate love had taken seed in her brain. The wedding garments themselves spoke of the enfolding skin of a lover. The feverishness with which she lived these prenuptial days (it lasted almost two months) was something quite holy to observe. One day after school she would be looking for the perfect house (along the Rue de Racine it had to be) for her betrothed and herself to move into. And then to the local toyshop to buy a tiny key to hang from the ring at her waist. The key must be small enough to slip through the keyhole of whichever house she decided would be hers.

The next afternoon we would be searching the *petites écoles* for a girl-child enough like herself to become the future child she would nestle against her breast. A Maltese cross around her neck, a waist-silk cap upon her head. Everything had to be in order for the wedding.

'Have you thought about a husband?' My cousin Emmanuel broke the train of her thoughts as she sat in her pristine finery on our sofa.

'It might be anyone except you,' she replied and meant it.

Giselle told me she had found the key that opened the secret door to her body and she and her fiancé made love four times a night in her own rumpled bed. My mother asked me if my friend was quite herself and I assured her she was. Giselle was not going to wait for marriage as girls are supposed to do. She said marriage could wait upon her. And so it did.

Thinking back I can see that my friend was doing what I would do in the convent years later when I lived my dreams in my imagination. The only difference was that Giselle always did everything much sooner and more quickly than I did. After several weeks of listening to her declarations about the joys and disappointments of married life (my friend was living in some country of the mind where fortunes daily flared then flagged), Giselle told me she had left her husband because he had accused her of never washing or changing her clothes. Looking at the soiled wedding garments (how much of *original* love she had sewn into them) I found myself in sympathy with her pretend husband.

Giselle took off her wedding clothes and packed them away in a small tin trunk she used to keep her toys in. Then she went to bed and slept for three days, waking every now and then to check the time on a treasured pocket watch hidden under her feather bolster. When she revived from these slumbers she told me she'd had her true love and was now ready to embrace whatever the real world held in store for her.

I nodded, not really understanding but never once doubting she knew her own mind. Giselle had always had the capacity to know instinctively what I could only ever learn by experience. When she did marry, three years later, wearing traditional green (which has always been the colour daughters of orchardists wear on their wedding days in Provence), she insisted her little trunk of grey lace and soiled silk accompany her to the altar and be placed between her and Philippe as they exchanged their bridal rings. It was her second marriage, she said. The first had been a trial run. Had she not had her preparatory marriage, she might have destroyed the later one with the intensity of the first.

Giselle betrayed me only once before she met Philippe. While I played sonatas relentlessly, oblivious to her presence, she knelt behind me and sewed my skirt and petticoat to the seat of the harpsichord stool. When I got up my clothes were ripped from my body there where I stood. It was a forewarning perhaps, for every thread of me was going to tear in the transition to womanhood.

When Giselle married Philippe she was already carrying his child in her womb. On their wedding day she wore the doll's house key on a chain around her neck so as not to draw attention to her expanding waistline. As her waist expanded so their love expanded too. I no longer saw my friend alone. I no longer saw my friend very often at all. I wanted some of their nectar for myself but I knew they weren't going to share it with me. When I met Giselle in the street her eyes were shining like freshly minted coins.

Back then I was not even conscious of my jealousy. I was only aware of a change in the nature of things which was not of my own making or desire. A numbness encircled my heart, a fog descended over my brain and I continued to live my life as though my friend and I were still together. Perhaps I could have forgiven Giselle had I thought Philippe worthy of her love, but I found his character inferior to hers. I disliked in particular his propensity for bombastic speech. He was attractive in that lean haggard sort of way young women often find irresistible, as though they seek the opposite of their own smooth skin and dimpled curves. Giselle found him very attractive, but needless to say he didn't appeal to me.

Once I sat in the fork of a tree and watched them make love in the summer grasses only twenty yards from me. I think they saw my face through the leaves. I think they knew I was a silent spectator on their passion. They had walked around the tree, arms entwined. They were laughing when they tumbled and fell in the dandelion-strewn grass. I wanted to run from the field, run all the way home, but I didn't want to be seen leaving. I didn't want Giselle to know I was hugging my loneliness to my chest in a wooden tree. By the time I made up my mind to leave, their lovemaking had begun and I was forced to remain where I was.

Why did they want me to see their pleasure? Perhaps Giselle wanted to educate me. To puncture my naivety. There was vanity in it too. The warm, gregarious vanity of lovers. They wanted to pull me close, then push me away. There was the contrast in it. My unhappiness. Their happiness. In the knowledge of my misery they could enjoy their own coupling more exclusively. (And I would not be able to appreciate the degree of their attachment until I had seen the consummation of their union first-hand.)

I watched without erotic gratification. Afterwards, because of the shame, I knew I would never be able to look at either of them again in the same way. When they departed I hung upside down in the tree as I used to do as a child, my legs looped around a horizontal branch. I saw the world as God must see it when he leans over to inspect our confusion more closely. I saw a mule and a foal with their heads in the hands of the sun. I saw the bark of my face reflected in the trunk of the tree.

I experienced a sensation of equilibrium hanging upside down, so that when I finally returned to the ground I was no longer thinking of Giselle and Philippe. They seemed only a very tiny corner of the tapestry of the world that was to be mine from that day on. I began to build a fence around our common ground. To derive protection from the gulf that separated us. I drank of the wind, of their absence, and the wind filled me up and whispered in my ear that I could do without bread and water.

Six months later, when Giselle went into labour, I was called to her bedside. The chains round my heart snapped one by one when I noticed Philippe's absence. Oh he wasn't there! He couldn't be there even if he wanted to. Yet still I feared he would pop up among us, a ubiquitous grinning jack-in-the-box.

We all loved Giselle too much to put her child's life before hers. After twenty-four hours the midwife knew the baby had died but she didn't dare tell Giselle's mama or me.

The doctor came into and went out of the room like a cold draught.

He knew.

Now it was just a question of whether Giselle had the strength to rid her body of the dead child.

On the second night her waters broke. They broke as they often do just before a baby is about to be born, with a huge force, gushing out and spraying everyone standing in the vicinity of the bed on which she crouched. Giselle's waters broke and continued to break. Hot springs burst from her. Her life's blood gushed out.

(It was as though she had been inhabited all along by a spirit of the deep.)

The water leaving her body changed in consistency and colour. First it had been the rosewater of the womb, which thickened and darkened to become her blood. Then it was the wild froth of her humours followed by musky rivulets of love, the freshwater of rivers and the salty brine of the sea. It was as though her body evacuated all the fluid there ever was in it and, after doing so, began to draw on all the waters of the world. (The Mediterranean, the Nile and the Indian Sea.)

Perhaps my friend had always been connected to the waters of the world. Their tides were her tides. Their songs her sea shanties.

Did Giselle feel the sea rushing through her body as she died? Did she know her blood turned the colour of mud and smelt of the Rhône? The doctor, the midwife and I were wading around the room, muttering pleas to merciful Mary.

It was so like my friend, I thought later, to die with such a passionate outburst of self.

Afterwards her empty body lay on the bed, the skinned hide of a young animal. Her face seemed flatter than normal, though the bone structure was more proudly defined than ever. Her pregnant belly was no longer in evidence, the child no longer within. We searched the waters for a floating body — perhaps we had missed the birth of the child in the preceding torrents. But no floating baby amongst the seasoned froth and placental weed was ever found. We could only assume the baby had turned itself back into water, into its compositional elements. Everyone knows a baby's bones are as soft as chalk.

I didn't hold Giselle after she died for there was nothing recognisable to take in my arms. All that was left to us were her bones with a wrinkled blanket of skin lying across them, a few sizes too big for what she had become.

I did not blame Giselle for marrying Philippe or bearing his child. These were her needs, not her failings. (Given another set of circumstances things might have turned out well.) I blamed her for dying and not knowing she was dying. Her ignorance in the face of her own tragedy. Could she not have spoken a word before the waters broke from her?

Could she not have clutched at a hand or cried out for help?

While the blood spurted from her she still had that expectant look on her face as though everything was going to be alright. As though *living* waters were carrying her child towards her at that very moment.

Had she known they were *dying* waters she might have stopped the bloodstream before it was too late. She was powerful enough to do that, even after two days of harrowing labour.

But she assumed the worst was over. She died almost rudely, mistaking death for birth.

I was left with a wound the size of which I did not know how to tend.

Now I know.

I know wounds can be tended like a garden, plot by plot, slowly and persistently, so that eventually the emptiness is replaced with new seeds of life. If I had known this then, I would not be the woman I am now. I would not have entered the Carmelite convent.

My mother and father tried to dissuade me. They offered to take me to Paris with them. I was their only daughter and they didn't want to give me up to God.

I told them they could visit me in the cloister every week if they wanted to. I knew it sounded cruel but I said it anyway. When they first saw me behind the grille they wept. (Even my father and I'd thought only music could make *him* cry.)

I refused to tend my wound, clinging to memories of Giselle instead. I preferred to hunger rather than heal. In 1783 I entered the convent an emotional child, and ten years later I departed still a child, determined that in my life to come I would avoid following in Giselle's footsteps. My mistakes would not be hers.

3

Emmanuel's

Water Music

*I*n the convent I discovered that music and emotion were one and the same thing.

Each instrument in our chamber orchestra represented a feeling we sisters were encouraged to suppress or master as we advanced towards God. The violins were romantic love, the flutes happiness, the oboes desire, the clarinets envy, the harp pleasure, the bassoon anger, the viol sadness, the trumpet impetuousness, the harpsichord fear, the triangle inspiration and the double bass lust. (The Reverend Mother didn't call the double bass lust though, she called it growing pain, but we knew what she really meant.)

When Mother Thérèse conducted us she would only ever refer to the instruments as emotions. 'A little more from you, Happiness; a little quicker, Desire; keep the scherzo in time, Envy; and don't rush that last bar, Fear.'

I got to know myself as Fear for it was the harpsichord I played in our small orchestra. I thought of myself as Sister Fear and became more fearful than I have ever been in life. I broke cups, stuttered responsorial psalms and woke in a sweat from bad dreams. I tried to learn the flute as quickly as possible so that I could think of myself as Happiness and walk with the light-footed steps of my flute-playing sisters.

The Reverend Mother said, 'When you have truly received *happiness* you will long for *sadness*. All must be experienced then denied.' I had a lot of instruments to learn, that was for sure. When we played together it made living in a convent seem worthwhile, but I kept my love for the music secret. Mother Thérèse might think my attachment constituted idolatry and deprive me of that along with everything else.

As Sister Fear I went to sleep with the sound of the harpsichord tinkering tremulously somewhere in my brain while my heart was thundering away inside the galleys of my chest. I went to sleep making a list of all the things that frightened me, the gong of my heart at the head of the list. Sister Desire lying next to me said I was supposed to come to the realisation that I was most frightened of myself. That's what the Reverend Mother wanted to hear anyway.

'Now you've spoilt it for me,' I complained.

'Help me with mine then.'

Remembering Giselle and Philippe I told my oboe-playing sister that desire could be mastered quite easily. One need only consider the destructive consequences resulting upon those infected by it.

Sister Desire shook her head. 'It's no use. That's fear talking and you can't help me today.'

Each morning, after pater, ave and credo were said in our chapel, Sister Patrice would ask me what I was most afraid of. I would say things she expected me to say, like making an enemy of God or of another sister. Once I told her childbirth was the thing I was most afraid of and she nodded for the first time. The next evening she asked me why, but I said I didn't know. She said I couldn't join the flautists unless I told her. One day I found the courage to tell her about Giselle. She listened intently and when I finished my story she told me Giselle was a part of myself and I should look after her whichever way I could.

'Do you mean as if she's still alive?'

'Yes,' said Sister Patrice. 'You must bring her back to life. Then you will know the happiness of the flute.'

In the convent I discovered that music was my right hand and emotion my left hand and never was a couple more meant for each other than they.

'Music is the whole world,' I said emphatically to Sister Desire while she was cleaning the inside of her oboe with a flannel cloth.

'If you're Monteverdi maybe. I'd call it a diversionary pleasure myself.'

I knew there was something false about nuns in the convent mastering emotions they were never going to experience in a real life. Lust, envy, desire, happiness even, were never spoken of as anything but aspects of the musical instruments to which we had been assigned and under whose influence we came whilst we were learning them. We were only allowed to experience these emotions in a frostbitten, one-hand-tied-behind-our-backs sort of way. Our own emotions were relics to be gazed at beneath a glass encasement. We could *play* our emotions, we could express them to bring joy to others in feast-day concerts, but we couldn't come close to knowing them in our own terms.

I had just begun savouring my appointment as Sister Happiness, playing the flute alongside two other sunny countenances, when I was told I had to move along and start learning the violin. I had been feeling on top of the world imagining our host-bearing chaplain dispensing *happinesses* in daily instalments to the tips of our tongues. Many nuns could play five or six instruments well and I had no particular objection to learning another, but I experienced an overwhelming resistance to learning the violin. Any instrument but that one, I told the Reverend Mother.

I wasn't going to explain to her right away that my cousin Emmanuel was a virtuoso violinist and our relationship had foundered upon the very emotion of *romantic love* the violin was supposed to represent in our home-grown orchestra. While Giselle had been frolicking around Avignon muddying her beloved wedding clothes, I had been fending off the advances of my Parisian cousin Emmanuel, who visited us every summer with his mother, my aunt Eloise.

'Why should I leave the kingdom of my girlhood for these tears and humiliations?' I asked Emmanuel, thinking about the boy across the road whom I'd invited to afternoon tea the previous year. The boy had accepted hesitantly and I'd waited expectantly with my tableload of treats. I waited all afternoon but he never turned up.

That summer (the same summer Giselle went wild over her wedding trousseau) Emmanuel was very open and friendly towards me. He touched me with his violin. His bow brushed against me. At every opportunity his body made contact with mine. I neither encouraged nor dissuaded him because I wasn't sure whether I liked it or not.

Why wasn't I sure? Giselle would have been sure, one way or the other, but her example was in part cautioning me because she seemed so out of control. 'You have to go mad to love another,' I declared to my cousin when we were on our way home from a Rameau opera. Emmanuel had sat beside me in the crowded theatre with a musical score on his knees, writing down the first violin parts as he heard them so he could play them himself the following day. (My father could always get us free tickets to see the Avignon performances because he was a close friend of the conductor.)

'That's the child who's scared of the dark speaking,' Emmanuel eventually replied, and I did not dispute this. He had wakened me to love before I was ready for it. He was seventeen and I was fourteen and he had a name for what he was feeling but I did not. It is necessary to have a name for one's exceptional feelings in order to manage them with confidence and offer them to others with civility.

My cousin usually listened attentively to my various explanations for refusing him, even though my excuses often changed from day to day. Normally he preferred to listen to the rise and fall of my voice rather than to the meaning of my words. I knew he did this because he would sometimes ask me to repeat what I had said when I demanded a specific response from him. Emmanuel's ear was tuned for sounds to the exclusion of everything else and one of his theories was that if we could all play a musical instrument proficiently we wouldn't need to waste time with words.

'If you bottle up your feelings, you *will* go mad,' Emmanuel warned.

'I do not think you would be able to take care of me,' I said another time, searching for practical reasons. He smiled without warmth. No, taking care of me was not something he particularly wanted to do. Perhaps his mother could look after me.

'Can Giselle come and live with us in Paris too?' I asked.

Later, after two holidays of rejections, Emmanuel became indirect and elusive. Occasionally he would even be antagonistic. It was his way of protecting himself, though I did not realise this at the time. I tripped over a wire which had been placed outside my bedroom door. Accusing my brothers of committing this crime I was shocked when Emmanuel confessed he had placed the wire there. He defended himself, saying, 'Why should I always be nice? *You're* not.' I was too embarassed to reply and chose to ignore similar incidents that followed.

My feelings for my cousin were trapped inside me. I dreamt again of my mother drowning in our backyard well and when I awoke from this nightmare I ran downstairs to check she was safe. 'Look after yourself tomorrow,' I explained as Mama tossed and turned beneath her patchwork quilt, annoyed at my midnight interruption.

My feelings for Emmanuel existed, I know this now but I didn't know it then. I even imagined my dreams might be reflecting an earlier attachment to the boy across the road, or my grieving for a friend of Julian's — a quiet and reflective child with grey-green eyes, who died a month after returning with us from a pilgrimage to Lourdes.

Unexpectedly at the age of sixteen (shortly after Giselle first met Philippe), my feelings for Emmanuel surfaced and they were like a volcano erupting inside me. Where had they come from, these mighty emotions? Giselle's feelings for Philippe were not of this kind, for they did not trouble her at all. If I let my feelings out they could destroy me, that's what I imagined. I would become Emmanuel and there would be nothing left of me. If he knew how I felt, my cousin would stop wanting me for sure. I longed for

Emmanuel to go back to Paris so that I could fantasise about him safely from a distance.

I did not expect my final rejection (which occurred when I had reached a legally marriageable age) would end his summer vacations with my family. I chose to continue with the existing harmony of my life and imagined the future would take care of itself. Giselle did not know she was dying when she was about to die and I did not know I was capable of loving Emmanuel.

Life's grand decisions are often made in distraction and haste. At the time one is only half aware of what is at stake. In the convent many sisters told stories of unfulfilled love. Repeatedly, distractedly, they unwound their tales till we learned not to listen. Unfulfilled love is the most long-lasting for it is composed of faith, hope and love in equal portions, the imagination shoring them together, keeping the past flickering on year after year.

Emmanuel and I could not get over our love because we had not lived it. Had we lived it, then it would have dissolved slowly, as love always does. It would have dissolved without leaving a taste of bitterness.

I refused to learn the violin and was confined to my cell for a week as punishment. Instead I began making a tiny violinist and violin to add to the figurines populating our miniature city of Avignon. Because our order was cloistered we depended on a century-old model of the town to refresh our memories of how the real place looked. The buildings were made of thick paper, painted card and various textiles discarded from the quilting room.

There was a river, a bridge and just about every building and street in the real Avignon. The Rhône, which I liked to stroke clandestinely when the other sisters weren't looking, was a rippling piece of indigo silk. The papal palace, with the cardinal and five bishops standing on each tower, had been constructed over fifteen years on the basis of our chaplain's drawings of the monumental edifice. Every detail was exactly in place. Terracotta roof, turreted towers, even the grime painted on the walls was exactly the colour it is, the colour of dried leaves. These walls had been constructed out of chips of living rock with real cement binding them together. Our own convent stood in the Place des Carmes with twelve ebony figures (mock hemp habits pulled over their heads) looking out of twelve open windows. The ebony figures were the sisters of course. They were us. You could open the door of the chapel and see the chaplain officiating at his altar. You could see our fat-faced cook ladling broth in the downstairs kitchen.

The convent was the one building our nuns had made interior rooms for. This delicate web of secret rooms with furnishings (including a minuscule orchestra carved out of nutshells) had only been completed a few years ago and was still in a state of alteration and repair, as was the whole model township. Its survival depended on a constant degree of maintenance which was mostly performed by a designated caretaker, Sister Marguerite. Each day Marguerite would take the twelve sisters for a walk along the Pont Saint Benezet. (She carried us in the palm of her hand. She let us walk freely along the bridge.) We would stop at the papal palace and talk to the real bishops (purloined chess figures, though not always bishops for bishops) who would fly down from their towers to greet us. They would deign to speak to us and we would humbly deign to reply.

So deprived of communication with men were we that these pantomimes brought tears to our eyes and sometimes we'd ask Sister Marguerite if we could postpone the walk home (in the palm of her hand) so we might accept an invitation from the courteous bishops to enter their papal home and acquaint ourselves with their regal rooms.

Sister Marguerite always refused. She was in charge of the model city and despite her timid ways she liked to exert the power which derived from her important responsibility in our little company of women.

When my cousin Emmanuel wanted to tease me and my brothers he used to say Avignon was only a storybook town. It wasn't a real town like his own city Paris. It was a pretty doll's house with a good-for-nothing bridge, a hopeless, popeless palace and medieval walls so tempting, urchins were climbing over them whenever they could.

Emmanuel would fetch his violin so that we might listen to the sound of the old bridge breaking (by a flooding Rhône), the Pope being carried back to Rome in his lurching litter, and medieval marauders climbing over the walls in their hundreds.

I had to ask Sister Marguerite's permission to include my figurine of Emmanuel in our hand-made city. She blessed and baptised my miniature cousin with a shy smile and agreed he might take his place amongst the scattered brethren. I put Emmanuel in a little boat on the silk-spun river and tucked his violin under his chin. I made a wish and said a real prayer for his safety in Vienna where I last heard he was living. I received no direct correspondence from him, but every couple of years his mother (still resident in Paris) sent me a handwritten score of an opera by Wolfgang Amadeus which my cousin had copied for us, knowing how much we admired the maestro's work.

When the tiny violin fell out of the figurine's arms onto the river Sister Marguerite picked it up and applied adhesive to hold it under Emmanuel's chin. 'All the sisters' great loves are here,' she told me somewhat breathlessly. How did she know I felt like that about my violinist? She pointed to various figurines. Here was Genevieve's army officer stooping over his rifle outside the papal barracks. Sister Catherine's student with an open journal sat on an apartment rooftop. Eloise's bearded Spaniard was sipping coffee in the Rue Carnot. Over there was Sister Blanchette's marquis in a yellow waistcoat, hands in pockets, and Beatrice's cotton trader sat in an apple-sized carriage rolling his way inconspicuously out of the gates of our model town.

'I didn't know it was love,' I said, not wanting to disappoint her. 'He was just my cousin.'

She laughed. 'None of them knew,' she said. 'No, no. It's much better to save love up for when it's all over.'

I could have cried.

'Would escape be possible?' I asked this of Sister Catherine as she lay in the bed beside mine, just before we went to sleep.

'Possible, but unthinkable,' she replied, pulling the blanket over her ear and closing her eyes.

All these sisters who knew what I was thinking, were they thinking the same things? I found consolation in the writings of Saint Teresa of Avila. 'The water of Thy grace,' she wrote, 'was not yet flowing beneath all this sand to stir it up.'

That night I dreamt of swimming violins. The reeds brushing against the strings. The water making its own music.

Giselle and I can't have been much older than fourteen when we were invited by Emmanuel to board a small fishing boat and, being handed an oar each, were assigned the strenuous task of rowing a boat full of musicians slowly up the Rhône whilst they played a scaled-down performance of Handel's *Water Music*, scored for eight instruments rather than the usual fifty. Emmanuel sat in the raised prow of the boat, one of his feet beating against a footrest, conducting and playing his violin at the same time.

'A bit like mixing a giant cake, isn't it?' Giselle commented as her oar dipped into the murky waters.

The rhythm of our oars had become an integral part of the music for if we did not pull together some of the musicians skipped a beat or fell behind.

Upon the water the instruments reverberated in an unexpected way. The cello sounded more like the French horn and the horn itself acquired an eerie high-pitched quality like that of a siren singing on a far-off island.

A river god was blowing through the music.

The instruments were becoming river instruments, anchored by the depth of the water beneath us and seasoned by the damp air circulating within and around them. It was Handel we were hearing, but a windswept and tattered Handel, pathetic at times — a majesty weeping for a missing crown.

We were listening to the strangling of a great beauty but notwithstanding this the music carried far and wide for they spoke of hearing us in the inland villages, across the river in Villeneuve-les-Avignon, and even as far away as Notre-Dame-de-Grâce.

'There was a weird tinkling sound and most of us heard it,' reported one villager. 'The children ran down to the blacksmith's cottage to see if he was making horseshoes ring and chime but he wasn't, so we knew it had to be something else.'

My cousin said he wanted to tune the Rhône so that slight sharpness in our instruments (a phenomenon which had something to do with the proximity of water and the fluctuating tide) could be redressed. Yes, he would tune the river for it had become the dominant instrument and our guiding hand. Giselle and I were instructed to keep the boat within the channel for the deepest waters produced the richest sound.

The musicians learnt to plumb the river's depths. They dropped anchors, measuring the distance from the surface to the bottom, then tuned their instruments accordingly. The wind players harnessed the prevailing winds, catching the currents in the shell-like cavities of trumpet and horn, then played more softly than was their custom.

For the strings it was a different matter. On windy days there was nothing to do but play with greater force, but on those rare calm days Emmanuel's violin reigned supreme. The other musicians stopped playing so they could listen, for my cousin had harnessed river and sky to the strings of his fiddle. He was playing the elements for us and an orchestra of fifty could be heard in the strands of his song.

In the convent when my mind broke open it was as though every sister in our chamber orchestra was playing her own tune as loudly as she could. Each instrument had become a weapon to use against the others.

Emotion had forgotten its mother tongue (the only true lover of women is music, says a wise old sage) and settled for Babel instead. The mastered and ignored demanded satisfaction. The Reverend Mother said it wouldn't have happened if I'd started learning the violin when she'd told me to. Making the model of Emmanuel for our little city hadn't helped either. When she told me these things she had to shout for my heart was thumping like the timpani in our midst. 'Go home to your mother,' she yelled and I thought she said 'Go home to your lover', which sounded obscene coming from her.

In our chamber music chapel, pages from a broken Bible sat on the music stands instead of Telemann's *Passion*. The nuns were reading the words like notes upon a musical score; they were making up jarring chromatic tunes to go with the tales. Those sisters who were my friends came into my cell to offer me solace then ran out again with their hands covering their ears. I chewed on countless keys and went from door to door rattling the locks with these spittle-covered clefs des champs. Defeated each time, I would knock politely and invite myself in as though nothing was wrong.

One of my eardrums burst. That was a relief because deafness was preferable to noise. The pain distracted me from my own distraction.

When the mistral paid us a visit, I stood on the cloister lawn and let the violent master wind twirl me like a weathervane, round and around and around. The cold blast from the Massif Central was funnelling its way along the valleys of my habit, whipping at my haunches and lifting my veil so high it danced against a cloud-free sky.

I knew the raging draught of cold dry air would be capsizing shipping and making ponds and lagoons in the countryside foam. I could feel it throwing people against the walls of buildings. I could see it dragging Roman tiles off roofs. I could hear it making the bells in the steeples ring without sacristan assistance.

I knew I should go indoors but on this day the wind was my saviour for I could no longer hear the fury of my heart.

The mistral had paid us a visit on the river too, ending our season of *Water Music* voyages. On that day, long ago, Emmanuel told Giselle and myself to tie ourselves to the mast with the anchor rope. The musicians attempted to bring the boat to shore but the river already held us in its writhing grasp and the force of the mistral made any kind of movement difficult. The yodelling wind filled our mouths and stifled all speech. The larger instruments were thrown about the boat, battering and bruising us, while the smaller ones blew overboard.

Not a drop of rain fell on us. The storm was a dry one and the sun shone heartlessly throughout the tempest. We were drenched from our feet upwards. The bottom of the fishing boat was six inches deep in water before we knew it.

I found myself wrapped around one person after another, in a clumsy dance sequence orchestrated from above. My arms were thrown high then dragged down low. I was clutching Giselle's arm which turned into Honoré's bassoon. He was gripping his instrument as furiously as I was. We were almost fighting over it!

I found myself in Emmanuel's arms. His body was rigid, the body of someone who thought he might drown. I became conscious of his breathing and I remembered he'd never been taught to swim. The wind threw us apart and I found myself clutching the mast again. When the wind died down we all found ourselves clinging to it as though it were a maypole.

I was not afraid of the windstorm. I'm not boasting. I was not afraid because I did not have a chance to think of myself. The elements were controlling us.

A number of instruments were lost to the river but Emmanuel's violin somehow ended up in my possession. When we were safely back on land I found it inside my coat, lying across my breast as warm and dry as a baby.

'What will you do without your bow?' I asked my cousin.

'A bow's not important. I can get another tomorrow.'

When we arrived home I went upstairs to change. My dress was soaked from the waist down to its dripping hem. I began to take it off. Between my dress and my petticoat, suspended down my spine, was the lost violin bow. I had perhaps been able to feel it there but hadn't noticed its presence until that moment when I saw the tip sticking out like a dislocated bone. I pulled the bow out quickly, expecting the wood to hurt as it rubbed against my spine, but the soft horsehair was facing inwards and it did no more than tickle.

During the windstorm Emmanuel's violin and bow had made a home for themselves on my person. In the mayhem of our shipwreck someone or something had opened my clothes and placed the instruments in those intimate places where I later found them.

If I had been able to express my gratitude to Emmanuel for loving me, he would have said, 'I have not loved you. The violin has loved you.'

The day I departed I remembered to thank the Reverend Mother and the sisters encircling her for loving me in the convent. I thought Mother Thérèse would say, 'God's will be done' or 'Mary's love it was'. She surprised me by asking my forgiveness for not having been able to make me love them enough. I could tell from her expression she believed she had failed me in some way. I certainly felt I had failed her and all the other nuns too. Perhaps people always blame themselves when love doesn't work out.

Perhaps they always feel like that.

Newly released from my vows, I walked around our town in a state of perturbed and very doubtful grace (is there any harder task than curing one's own complaint?) returning to the places I had known as a girl, remembering one thing after another.

I looked around for the characters in Marguerite's model city and found them (or most of them) in the exact positions she had placed her cherished figurines. I christened them anew, from the tongues of the jilted and still-yearning. Rogues they were, most of them, an insight I suddenly found thought-provoking.

Then I saw a young man walking along with a violin case strapped to his back. He might have been Emmanuel. From the bridge I saw a boatload of fishermen, their baskets resting between their legs like musical instruments. When I climbed Castle Rock and looked out over our township's canopy of pink roofs I became anxious about the enormity of my freedom. I put my hand to my throat several times and felt its nakedness. I gripped the stone wall with my other hand, stifling an immense desire to throw myself over the cliff.

A hundred feet below, the river danced and rippled like a field of silver rye. The fishermen dipped into it, knowing their Grail. I put my hand to my throat, and listening to the soothing music of a nearby fountain, I felt strong enough to walk on.

Part 2

Transition

Sur le pont d'Avignon
On y danse on y danse
Sur le pont d'Avignon
On y danse tout en rond

Traditional French Song

4

The Dance Academy

of Avignon

*T*here is a ruined château perched high on a hill not far from Avignon. My family used to picnic every year in the valley below to celebrate my mother's birthday. An emerald green river runs through the village. It spurts from its source in a fountain of bubbling sonnets and whirlpools of delirious content.

We children would climb the hill and play inside the broken walls of the medieval castle. The sky was its only roof, the ground crumbled underfoot and we would wander around and pretend we belonged to the past. One year my brother Julian dressed up as Richard the Lionheart with a bow over his shoulder and a quiver of arrows on his back. The arrows were made from Emmanuel's discarded violin bows for he practised so much he wore one out every month.

When Constantine and Emile started fighting over these wooden arrows I had to take them away. I put them back in the quiver and slung it over my shoulder for safekeeping. My seventeen-year-old cousin had climbed the side wall of the castle and was walking along its upper ledge. He wasn't allowed up there. None of us were. (The drop was five hundred feet down a sheer cliff and the ledge he was walking along was less than a foot wide.)

I said nothing for I didn't want my brothers to notice him. They might think they could do this too. I led the boys down the hill telling them it was nearly time for birthday cake. Returning to the confines of the château and trying to sound nonchalant, I told my cousin not to fall if he could possibly help it.

'Why not?'

(Emmanuel. This isn't funny you know. Get down from there at once.)

'Don't you care if I die?'

I could no longer look. I turned away. Then I heard a crunch of stones underfoot and he was at my side calling me Mademoiselle Lionheart, almost gloating as he asked me if I realised I loved him when I thought he might die.

When he was walking along the ledge I *had* felt a mixture of fear and desire for Emmanuel, but the latter was at the expense of my respect for him. In response to his question I pulled an arrow out of the bag and struck him hard across the arm with it. Emmanuel looked surprised. He grabbed me roughly by the waist and pulled a bow-arrow out for himself. I thought he was going to strike me and I moved away in self-defence, but the ground was uneven and I fell backwards onto rubble and weed-strewn rocks. My cousin laughed. Not nervously, cruelly. The anger emptied out of me straightaway. I couldn't feel anything for him. I picked myself up, trying to imagine what Giselle would say if she were here. She would know what to do.

Emmanuel was tapping the bow against his open hand. 'Well, aren't you going to fight with me, Marie-France?'

'Yes, I can fight,' I replied after a long pause, 'if there's something worth fighting for.' And biting my lower lip I turned and walked out of the château without looking back.

When I left the Carmelite convent memories I'd pushed away long ago came floating back. I caught them in my hands and they stung like bees to repay me for forgetting them.

With pollen on the palms of my hands I began to brush-mend the cracks in my head.

In the convent I'd been thinking about Emmanuel on the river, the musical Emmanuel who was gentle and considerate. Thrown back into the world outside I kept remembering the other Emmanuel who'd wanted to cause me pain. The cousin I still cared about was the good Emmanuel and the cousin I desired was the bad Emmanuel. This conflict made me unsure about writing to my cousin and telling him I was no longer living in a cloister. I didn't want to marry the bad Emmanuel and I doubted I could make him go back to being the cousin who possessed no hatred of me.

In my father's music shop, working on the harp, I saw my cousin's shadow lurking behind each of the larger instruments, half revealed, stretching upwards as though struggling to be born of the violoncellos and pianofortes themselves. As I mended the harp I knew my mind was healing too. I felt less fragile walking around our town. I no longer had to hide behind pillars when carriages rushed past.

In the workroom, surrounded by so many instruments, there never was a quieter, more silent place in the whole world. It was a relief when one of the instruments was purchased and taken away so that it might do what it had been made with such protracted labour to do.

My father was often brusque with me. 'You'd better hurry up and find a husband, you're not getting any younger,' he'd say. Even Mama became short-tempered. I'd say I was praying in my attic room but she wasn't fooled by these assertions of holiness. She gave me a list of chores every day and when I turned up my nose she said the convent had spoilt me.

They loved having me back for I was their security. On the surface I was clinging to them, but in hindsight I think it was Mama and Papa who didn't want to let me go. Papa encouraged me to accept invitations to dances, but he refused to pay for the fashionable new dresses I needed to look like a woman with a sizeable dowry to bring to a marriage. Mama had other ways of sabotage. She would always accompany me to the elegant homes and because she was charming and I used to be shy and awkward in company, the men were attracted to her and not to me. I admired Mama as much as the men did. She was young at heart.

I was sometimes invited to dance by men who told me I was pretty. I danced with a man who looked like Emmanuel six times in a row. I couldn't believe my luck the first two times — same figure, same smile, same nose. The third time he told me he'd never heard of Wolfgang Amadeus and the spell was broken. The fifth time I danced with him because I liked his smile and nose and the sixth time it was beginning to annoy me that he didn't have Emmanuel's eyes or voice, so I told him it would have to be our last dance.

In the carriage going home I told Mama I had informed the Emmanuel lookalike I was engaged to a man in Arles, and as much as I would like to continue dancing with him, it wouldn't be seemly to do so. Mama told me off for lying but I defended myself and said it was alright to lie when you were trying not to hurt another's feelings. Even Mother Thérèse said this was a forgivable sin. Mama said the Carmelite mother didn't know everything. Society might now hear I was engaged and I wouldn't be asked to dance by the earnest types with serious intentions.

Back home I took a candle up to my attic room and knelt as I was accustomed to doing, mumbling our familiar vesper prayers with renewed faith. I missed my Carmelite sisters. I missed the chamber orchestra but I knew they'd stopped the music since taking the legal oath. Deprived of the support of our patrons and of alms from the community, my fellow sisters had to live solely from the profits of their handiwork. The local revolutionary committee was trying to starve our cloistered orders into submission.

Sometimes I walked along the Rue des Carmes hoping to hear some singing from behind the walls. (I never did.) I saw soldiers drag our chaplain out and ferry him away. Then I heard the Reverend Mother scream. I couldn't see her but I heard her cry as though they were pulling out her tooth.

I ran away. I ran all the way home. I didn't see the bodies in the alleyways but when I reached our door I turned and saw my trail of footprints stamped with other people's blood.

The following week it became known my Carmelite mother had refused once and for all to secularise her convent. Dragoons had allegedly tortured her but still she wouldn't give in. Mother Thérèse and the other sisters wished to remain a contemplative order. As a consequence they had been ordered by the republican commissioners to leave our country or join the other papal loyalists in prison.

I wondered what they would decide to do.

An eruption of male carnal urges was to blame for the revolution, Mother Thérèse always used to say. 'It's all trumpets and double basses out there,' she proclaimed, describing the battles that were taking place in and around our river town. In 1791, at the time of the worst atrocities in Avignon — in particular a massacre in which one hundred and thirty men, women and even some children were murdered in the dungeons of our papal palace — the Reverend Mother advised us to stand firm and formally renew our vows to God and King. We did so in the presence of the parliamentary visitors from Paris who had come to offer us our liberty. The visitors were much more tolerant of our continuing beliefs in the first years of the revolution. They were prepared to compromise with us.

As conservative as the right hand of God, Mother Thérèse would prefer to go to the guillotine singing than consider the possibility of real change within our order. In the wealthy Cistercian convent on the other side of town things happened differently. (A city of women the abbess had always called it, a Cistercian 'citadel of love'.) When brigands stormed the convent the abbess made the three young novices hide inside the bells in the belfry so they wouldn't be raped. The brigands never thought of looking for them there. They desecrated holy icons and stole gold and valuable artwork from the chapel. When partial order was restored, the building became the legal property of our Avignon Academy of Dance. The authorities handed Pedrillo, a local dance master, the keys and told him to institute change as fast as he could. After the floor-to-ceiling mirrors were put up in the old dining room it was all over for piety and prayer.

Almost over, I should say. The abbess adapted to the new way of thinking while continuing to recite the hours and the rosary with her remaining sisters in private.

Passing the former Cistercian convent on my way to the market in the months following my release from the Carmelites, I would look in at the dancers through the windows, admiring their graceful gestures and the Grecian tunics they wore (slit down the sides so they could arabesque with ease). The former novices danced a dance of seven veils, still protecting their glistening spider-work of hair beneath the fraying head-frocks. They clung to their veils like children to nursery blankets they have long since outgrown.

They were nuns but not really nuns. I watched them genuflecting at the ballet barre, these sisters whose bodies were finally being taken into account. (It was as though they'd been wearing them inside out for years and no-one had bothered to tell them.)

They had never been like the Carmelites. The Cistercians subscribed to the teachings of Saint Bernard of Clairvaux, who had joined their order in the twelfth century and influenced them greatly. While Mother Thérèse was telling her Carmelite daughters to deny the senses at all cost, the Cistercian abbess was encouraging her novitiates to descend first then rise, for in order to know Him better, God had lovingly implanted carnality within them. Saint Bernard believed categorically that love must begin with the flesh.

In our Carmelite convent we heard about the ritual flagellations on the other side of town. Mother Thérèse disapproved, but I knew the bodies of the Cistercians must have been more alive than ours. Hurting was a kind of feeling. There must have been some pleasure in it for them.

Playing hide-and-seek, at the age of nine, I raced into our music room and found a hiding place for myself under the lid of our fashionable new German pianoforte. My chest and belly were compressed against the fretwork of strings. I was just small enough to squeeze inside, but the lid wouldn't close entirely.

'Pretend I'm not here,' I told my cousin who was sitting at the keys, composing.

'You'll wreck the instrument,' he complained, but when my little brothers ran into the room calling out, 'Emmanuel, Emmanuel, have you seen Marie-France?' he started to play the pianoforte in a relaxed fashion and told them he had no idea where I was.

Because the lid was slightly raised I could see our baby Emile copying everything his brothers were doing as they flitted behind curtains and crawled under chairs. He hardly knew what he was supposed to be looking for but this didn't deter him (his face all cherubim dimples and smiles). Then the band of boys tore out of the room like a mob of Vandals, shrieking and jabbing at each other in the same undisciplined way they'd come in.

Emmanuel continued to play the pianoforte. I lay silently as the strings vibrated through my body. The taut wires were digging into my skin but I didn't care. My head was turned on its side. The strings of the instrument were leaving marks upon my flushed left cheek.

'Don't stop,' I told my cousin.

'Your papa will come in.'

But Emmanuel continued to play at my request.

The same evening at the dinner table I stood up on my chair and declared to all those present: 'My body rules the keys!' My cousin snorted. My mother and father looked slightly uncomfortable. I sat down quickly and bent my head for the blessing of food. A week or two later I remember seeing Papa patiently rewiring the strings of the pianoforte, but Emmanuel didn't tell on me. He was good like that. Cousins make better friends than brothers do. As lovers they're most desirable but it's so sticky you'd be better off boiling toffee from the syrup than cleaving to them and losing yourself in the mire of molasses they make.

On one of my strolls past the newly designated Academy of Dance in the bitter winter months of 1794, three former Cistercians appeared at a window above and dropped a long rope of plaited veils down to me. (Looking out at the world was no longer forbidden them.) I grasped the veils as the women intended me to do and they lifted me a foot off the ground.

They pulled harder and I floated in confused uncertainty, wrapping the soft rope around my waist, searching for security in the sandy crevices with my feet as I rose. In a few seconds I would be looking at them face to face. (Now I was climbing the wall on my own initiative.) In a minute they would be dragging me inside.

Curiosity drew me into their topsy-turvy world. Curiosity and a freedom grown so large it hung on me like a sack of boredom. I coveted the Athenian tunics they wore; I missed the stroke of a cowl upon my neck, and I still wanted to be told what to do. Mama and Papa were happy to tell me what to do, but I never felt I *had* to do what they advised. I knew them too well, and they perhaps loved me too well. After six months of living in each other's pockets we needed some time apart. The reformed Cistercian convent wasn't like a prison. There were no bars on the windows and I could go home again if I wanted to.

In the Academy of Dance there was safety and novelty and lots of rules. For a start we were not allowed to call the abbess Mother. She was simply Claude to us. She was running the school with Pedrillo, the Sicilian-born impresario who frequently danced on his toes and showed us stiff-limbed women how it could be done. He told us to stretch our limbs and consider our reflections in the gallery of mirrors to learn what we could from them. He advised us not to admire ourselves until we had reason to.

Then he instructed us to lose weight and lose weight and lose weight.

He had a passion for thin women and Marie-Françoise and Marie-Eloise, who starved themselves as part of their daily penance, had already become his favourites. He admired the curves of their ribs, the pointed shoulder blades and narrow twigs of legs.

Technical virtuosity would be theirs, Pedrillo claimed, likening them to a star of the Paris Opera, Madeleine Guimard, also known as La Squelette des Graces.

I kept expecting Pedrillo to don a soutane and turn himself into a priest. It seemed odd not to have one around. None of us quite trusted him. If we desired him we loathed ourselves for doing so, knowing there was something intrinsically bad about the man who was tempting us. We admired him when he was demonstrating Beauchamp's five positions of ballet and detested him as soon as he walked off the polished floor.

'He's a goblin-man again!' My new friend Angelica came running out of the refectory with her dance slippers slung over her shoulder. Pedrillo came loping after her, his long hair pinned up, exposing an exquisitely beautiful neck. When he danced he was charismatic but when he walked he was a little ungainly, as though his body was quite happy to deny in its normality the beauty of the springs that lived within it.

'Angelica ate two desserts,' Pedrillo complained with barely controlled derision.

'I'll tell her off later,' I said to keep him on side. Then I walked past him into the refectory and ate two desserts myself, just to spite him. I kept looking around to see if his face would appear at the door. Part of me wanted him to appear and part of me didn't want to see him again.

After ten years as a nun my head usually presided. Reason insisted that my bodily desires, were I to act upon them, would prove themselves dirty, demonic and detrimental to my health. There were twenty other dancers Pedrillo had to oversee, so I don't expect he wasted a thought on me. I was never going to be a great dancer. The abbess had almost assigned me to the academy orchestra with the other musical nuns.

Our *maître de ballet* now focused exclusively on Marie-Françoise and Marie-Eloise as they rehearsed in the studio, forging some muscle into their brittle limbs. He advised them not to fast to excess and faint for he wanted their bodies strong, not weak. *Devant, à la seconde, derrière.* He never laid a finger on their sweating bodies as they swayed to and fro, their clammy palms sticking to the barre, their praying mantis arms and legs flexing in and out. Pedrillo was a professional dancer. It would have been sacrilegious for him to attempt a *mouvement de séduction* on the dance floor.

Off the floor? Well that was another matter.

The Cistercians who were turning into dancers were still too scared to go outdoors. To breach the cloister walls. They continued to look back at what they'd left behind. Their loyalty was to Claude, not Pedrillo. In the privacy of Claude's candlelit chamber, veiled in a mist of frankincense and myrrh, we tied up our dance tunics and flagellated ourselves. This, I decided, was fitting punishment for owning such strong desires in the first place.

Claude stood in the middle of our circle, twirling around like a dancer in a music box. She sang Ave Marias in the voice of a trained opera singer but there was one note she could never hit. There was a missing key in her voicebox and unfortunately this key was middle C. It had cost her a singing career many years before, but I didn't mind these mute gaps in her otherwise swallow-throated flight of notes. Her voice was angelic, a beatitude of beating wings, a self-love to aspire to. I couldn't help singing that quintessential note for her, filling the hole in her halo of hallelujahs.

Because there weren't any priests the former abbess said the Eucharist herself, and because there wasn't any wine on the premises she offered us milk from a glazed china bowl. When Claude began the familiar refrain: 'This is my body that I have given up to you ...' I knew it was her own body she was talking about and not God's.

When we drank milk from the bowl, I remembered my mother kneeling over spilt milk and broken china on our kitchen tiles, and I wanted to return home and lay my head in her lap.

Angelica and I were physically attracted to Pedrillo but we didn't like the person he was. We used to hide from him at the bottom of a dry well located in an enclosed forecourt of the old Cistercian convent. We climbed down a rusty ladder and sat on the dusty floor of the well. We crossed our legs and pulled our dance tunics tightly over our knees, pressing our shoulders together to spill our trusty confidences.

My young friend kept her home-made chocolates hidden behind a broken brick in the wall of the well. We would laugh hysterically at the thought of Pedrillo not knowing the chocolates were there. It used to infuriate him to see my *très gentille* friend arrive for afternoon dance class with a fine brown line pencilled just above her upper lip.

In the dry well Angelica told me she'd wanted to be a bullfighter for a long time. Her Spanish-born father had been a bullfighter. She'd seen him twist and turn in the arena at Arles until the strongest *taureau* in the land had run him through.

'But the bull made you an orphan,' I objected.

'I want to avenge my father's name,' Angelica explained.

She wanted to know if I had any unfulfilled dreams. I told her that since leaving the Carmelites I'd had sleeping dreams in which I found myself chattering away to someone I knew very well. I thought it might be my cousin Emmanuel, but I wasn't sure. When I woke I tried to remember what had transpired in the dream, but I could never capture any more than the fleeting voices, 'Is it time, is it time yet or must we wait for another life?', which made sleeping sometimes a tiring occupation.

'I have those dreams sometimes,' Angelica nodded. 'I'm with my parents again.'

'Do you ever dream about God?'

'No. But I dreamt about Jesus when I was a child,' she answered hopefully.

In the academy Angelica and I were becoming *danseuses* and leaving some of our devotions behind. Pedrillo's ballet routines were intruding into Claude's parlour. The two locations were merging into one. The former abbess clung onto the old order and we hung onto her, but anticlerical winds were sweeping us forward in time.

One evening Angelica startled us by using her whip as a skipping rope in the middle of Claude's Ave Maria. As we flagellated ourselves my friend spent ten minutes dancing in and out of her rope like girls in marketplaces do. The former abbess's power was being challenged. That was what was happening, though we didn't understand this at the time. When Angelica began her contrapuntal skipping dance we could no longer concentrate on the rhythmic beat of the ropes as they struck our bodies. Elisabeth started giggling, then she and Angelica tied their ropes together and began skipping in unison while Claude told us to ignore them and proceeded to sing on.

Shortly after this she gave in to our skipping whim herself, indulging in the novel practice (skipping for whipping) while we continued to take the sacrament from her in the customary fashion. We were no longer ashamed of our attachment to Claude's body and the milk of her body. We could enjoy her without feeling guilty about it. We saw Claude's priestly body offered to us as the exercise in charity it was. Our neediness and her mercy.

With our skipping ropes in our hands we were completely happy in her chamber for the first time, but it was a happiness like any other, which could not last forever, which would not last very long at all. As we skipped around Claude we felt our guilt rising to the ceiling along with the smoky tendrils of frankincense and myrrh. We had our bodies back and we had Pedrillo to thank, and Claude, and the music and each other too.

Now the abbess sometimes peered through the window of the dance studio as we pointed our toes and sweated and twirled. She was trying to estimate Pedrillo's power over us and see if it were possible to win us back. In our latter-day bewilderment we sometimes longed for her to do so. It was the thought of hurting the God I had cherished throughout my convent years that made me consider returning to Claude's fold. I could not fool myself that in turning away from Him I wouldn't suffer greatly.

But I loved my strong new body. If I had put my life into the hands of God too early I wanted to make up for it now. The muscles growing in my upper arms and calves were welcome to me. Even though I knew it was impossible, I aspired to be as thin as Marie-Françoise and Marie-Eloise. I stopped eating dessert and taking sugar with my coffee. At eight o'clock I would fall asleep from exhaustion, and Claude would reprimand me at matins for missing our evening prayers.

In the dance studio we seemed to be growing younger rather than older as we spun like tops across the shiny wooden floor. In the refectory Pedrillo continued to keep a watchful eye on Angelica's dietary habits, encouraging her to eat more fruit and vegetables and to abstain from drinking chocolate. One evening he placed a huge bowl of fruit and vegetables on the table in front of her and picked from it a *melon* and *concombre*. 'You must exchange this for this,' he said to Angelica, gesturing crudely with the produce in his hands. '*Melon pour concombre, melon pour concombre*. Most women do it with ease, though some prove resistant.'

Angelica blinked a few times.

'You're not going to, so why should we?' she eventually replied.

Pedrillo smiled smugly, 'That is the privilege of having been born a man in this world.'

My friend scowled. 'I'm never going to do that with you, you boggle-man,' she said. Then she grabbed the *melon* from his hand and ran from the room with it. 'I envy the Holy Mother her virgin birth,' Angelica confided to me late that night in the cell we now shared.

'I do too,' I replied, though it had never occurred to me before that I did.

Angelica let her hand stray against the cracked and blistered wall. Plaster she picked at fell upon the worn floorboards and broke into sugary anthills. She stood upright, grasping the frame of her metal bed in frustration, guiding it like a sleigh through snow.

'We're never going to dance on the Avignon stage, are we, Marie-France?'

I did not reply. Despite the desperation in my young friend's voice, I was not prepared to admit to her that the once appealing dance academy had outlived its usefulness after only a few months. I still wanted to make my debut on stage but the rational part of me knew this wasn't going to happen. The dance academy was merely a corridor leading to another room. It wasn't the large light-filled chamber I'd been searching for. I didn't want to be part of a community of women any more. I wanted to think as an *I*, rather than as a *we*. And it seemed pitiful we had only a man like Pedrillo to relate to.

That night I dreamt of joining the corps de ballet with Marie-Françoise and Marie-Eloise, only in the dream it was not a corps de ballet it was a corps of barren women, and instead of dancing on the Avignon stage we were pirouetting our way along a field of ruined corn.

When I departed the Carmelites it was my head that led the way, signalling its need for change. When I left the dance academy it was my body that made the decision for me. I found myself packing my trunk and thinking, so I'm leaving again, am I? I wanted Angelica to come with me but she was an orphan and would only leave when her spiritual mother Claude left too. Their bond had been too long-serving for it to be snapped in half overnight.

I left of my own free will, though my mind was only skipping after the interests of my recently awakened body. Now I was faced with a tremoring within, an anxiety-provoking bodily fugue or malady of sorts which I attributed to the changing modus operandi underway. I knew this condition could only be borne within the most trustworthy framework of faces, and I was keen to return to my family as soon as possible. Claude pressed me to her bosom in farewell, an action which would have been beyond the capabilities of Mother Thérèse.

'Have I descended enough to rise?' I asked, hoping she would not reject me for my own rejection of her world. She laughed mildly, implying I had merely a case of the jitters rather than a life and death affliction.

'Marry for love, won't you,' were her parting words and it was as though she had reached out her fingers and placed them against the pulse in my neck. So different from Mother Thérèse's final advice, yet both women had selected similar words to sum up my quandary.

Whom was I to trust? (Even then I knew it was possible they both spoke the truth.) Claude gave me a copy of Bernard of Clairvaux's *Treatise on the Love of God* to take home with me. I hid the seminal Catholic text up my sleeve until I had a private moment in my old attic room to read the words of the saint away from the eyes of the world. There were some now resident in Avignon who would throw his jubilatory gospel in the fire.

The book was fastened with a locked clasp but Claude had forgotten to give me the key. Perhaps it had long since been lost. I certainly had no intention of returning to the Avignon Academy of Dance to request it. I knew I had enough strength in my hands to break open the small lock. But would it not be a sacrilegious thing to do? To violently force my way into the blessed pages of a holy man?

Perhaps my first and strongest allegiance to our Carmelite founder, Saint Teresa of Avila, made its presence felt at this moment for I decided that I definitely could desecrate the cover of the book for the purposes of seeking active counsel within. Teresa would have done the same with the works of Saint John of the Cross if she'd had to. What was a cover anyway but a ruse, a dead skin to be sloughed off when the true spirit of thought inside was revealed to the discerning reader?

I broke open the lock with my bare hands, like a child breaking open walnuts. The book survived my attack on its binding, though the cover was spoiled for good. The pages fell open at a certain much-read page and the first words my eyes alighted on were these: *from that time on one is led to love God purely on account of a felt sweetness than of needed help.*

My heart, my head, my spirit, my flesh. United in a bodily transfusion of love. Nothing was left out. I heard echoes of my own thoughts in the unguent preaching of the French saint and, no longer caring for the security of darkness, I lit my night lantern, held it over the slim manual in my hand and read on.

5

The underwater

Almshospital

*T*here is only one hospital in Avignon which not so long ago used to be an almshouse. It is to the east of our town, just outside the ancient walls in a squalid quarter built over a canal and therefore subject to dampness and flooding. In winter our invalids are transported to the high ground of nearby Les Baux, but proximity to water has always been viewed as advantageous in summer, when the almshospital offers to the homeless and sick a hundred rickety well-made beds.

None of my family had ever been in the almshospital because we could always afford a doctor to come to our home. When I was very small Mama spent some time in Les Baux, recovering from a difficult confinement, but I don't think she convalesced with the other invalids. The only thing I remember clearly is our excitement when she returned, and how it was a warm sunny day even though Mama and Papa insist it was February and perhaps even snowing.

In 1780 an exceptionally severe flood caused canal water to enter the almshospital and overnight reach as high as the beams of the ground-floor lodgings. Canal water flooded the rooms where the invalids were sleeping, lifting up their mattresses and floating them from dormitory to dormitory on the swiftly ascending tide. Some of the sick apparently awoke to the sound of splashing and the sight of the formerly bedridden swimming around in search of their prized possessions: their handbags, wallets and tortoiseshell cases of tobacco and snuff.

Rather than moping about the misfortune, most of the homeless were amused by the sheer silliness of it all. In the days of mopping up which followed, almshospital staff became aware that the surfeit of water was having a beneficial effect on many invalids. In the oppressive July heat cooling waters could be applied to burning foreheads and swelling limbs. Ailments were more easily borne and more quickly recovered from. People's spirits simply rose as their mattresses had done when they floated free from the supporting structures of their metal frames.

As a consequence it was decided to utilise the system of canals running under the building and keep the almshospital permanently flooded. My brother Julian came home from Latin school with pages of fascinating architectural plans copied from chalk drawings done by his schoolmaster. Warm water would flow through boiling pipes from the basement of the almshospital, to be reheated in the kitchens above. A Roman system of pipes and leverages had been adapted by our local engineers who knew how to drain the bulging strongman of the Rhône.

I was curious to see inside the new building, and I took my brothers walking past the institution many a time. The street-level rooms were flooded almost to their ceilings, and through the windows we could observe various hospital personnel diving down to collect items of clothing, or belongings forgotten or lost to invalids upstairs. The floor was covered with broken crockery, worthless jewellery and discarded fruit stones, giving the appearance of the shelled floor of the sea. Everything unwanted was thrown from the first storey down to the ground level (through an old chimney shaft where excess water gurgled and shunted) but the objects looked different in their underwater state and were often mistaken for other things.

We could see fake pearls shining like real ones inside the oyster-shell clasps of buckled shoes. Oranges and lemons bobbed about on the surface, translucent as crystallised fruits, and were sometimes retrieved by domestics who would force open a door (water gushing into the outside corridor) and swim across the room to salvage these edibles.

Occasionally, by accident, ducks got caught up in the irrigation system and were seen having a ball of a time quacking away and braving the waterslides that connected one floor to the next. Adventurous as they always are, ducks usually made it onto the landing where domestics would find themselves walking upstairs and downstairs (through the waterfall of life) beside these webbed-footed visitors from the local canals.

Seeing my brothers and I watching on the other side of the glass the domestics would sometimes wave their oranges and lemons (holding their breath if they were fully submerged) and, bearing smiles, point upwards invitingly as if they hoped to meet us on the first-floor landing where the water was shallow enough to paddle in and the ducks well fed enough to embrace.

But there was no way into the underwater hospital unless one was prepared to help the sick return to health or fake a serious illness oneself, as some fascinated children or perverse adults had been known to do. The truly infirm were not in love with the underwater hospital of course. The water was merely the medicinal tonic that made them feel better, for when they entered they had never felt worse.

The almshospital was to become my first place of employment after my brief sojourn in the dance academy. The revolutionary government, so pleased with me for heeding their advice and leaving the beleaguered Carmelites, had now offered me a stipend to either teach or nurse, to become one of those daughters of the state, *une fille seculière*. I chose nursing because I was hoping the tremoring within might heal in a place of palliative care. Our family doctor diagnosed my shaking complaint as an after-effect of the more serious illness I had suffered in the Carmelite convent. He advised me to avoid marriage for the time being and to find an occupation that kept me busy but did not overly tax my nerves.

Entry into the underwater almshospital was dependent on my proven ability to swim rather than sink. Documentary evidence was provided by my Avignon baptismal certificate for the picture on the seal is a flounder's (also known as flatfish's) tail. The first requirement of any Rhônian mother or father is to teach their child to swim!

The hospital was run by a former Augustan sister now dressed in civilian clothes except for a veil wrapped around her head like a turban. She said the headdress was to protect her hair from the spray of waters and she gave me a new veil and showed me how to tie up my hair in a similar fashion.

'Like Mahometans,' I said.

'You have beautiful ears,' she replied, but I am partly deaf from when my right eardrum burst and as this was the ear she was speaking into I heard 'ears' as 'tears' and, putting my hand to my cheeks, could feel drops of spray there (from navigating the waterfall of stairs). I brushed these away with my sleeve, realising that in the almshospital moisture was going to be both friend and enemy, an image of a dry cave in lofty Les Baux already filling my mind as a desirable winter alternative.

Fearful as ever of human contact (and especially of catching a contagious disease) I told the sister I would be happy washing dishes but she laughed and said the old fire grates with their waterspouts washed all the dishes these days. She'd have to find something else for me to do.

Marie-Victoire, as I came to know her, was neither as conservative as Mother Thérèse nor as liberal as Claude. She had accepted the need to secularise the almshospital where she had been working as a religious sister for more than ten years. She had adjusted with ease to the new republican system of nursing and was happy in her position as matron and hospital supervisor, even if she was not always happy in herself. She liked things to be a certain way and if they didn't go that way she would explode with anger. While things were running smoothly she was a joy to work with — organised, cheerful and knowledgeable — but if something untoward happened, something she had no control over, she would react with an outburst of rage. She usually apologised, but still, the domestics were wary of working alongside Marie-Victoire.

The day I arrived in the almshospital she was in a very pleasant mood indeed. She told me to hold tight to the banister and we fought our way upstream to the second floor where the dormitories were located. Here I came face to face with invalids in beds which were floating around and banging into each other. The mattresses needed to be constantly reigned in and moored with ropes to the walls. (This was a job I could do for sure.) Ailments were treated with spoonfuls of cinnamon syrup (bringing smiles not frowns), and feathers were used to bind wounds because they were water-resistant and soothing as well. Some invalids had so many feathers stuck to them they looked like chickens, plumped up in their water beds and attending to each other's wounds with a plucking and stroking of quills. Blood-letting was out of fashion (there was enough blood-letting going on in the world outside, Marie-Victoire told me) so the feverishly ill and profoundly congested were covered with lilies and poppies then hypnotised by charmers who knew the trick of yawning in the faces of those they wished to lull to sleep. (Watching someone else yawn always makes you sleepy I too found out soon enough.)

Domestics in sealskin skirts, their whalebones compressed into propeller fins at the back, glided through the rooms as though they did this sort of thing every day of the week, which of course they did. They dispensed golden beer and loaves on trays, balancing them on their heads as African women do with water pots.

Marie-Victoire introduced me to every invalid and they each requested me to read newspapers to them. (This I discovered was to be my major employment in the almshospital.) Then the matron of the house took me up to the third floor where the water was warmest and shallowest and up to the shins only, for the elderly who disliked depth and for young children who would surely have drowned in deeper waters.

The invalids sat on the floor in the warm water (heated by pipes that flowed from the raging furnace in the basement below) having dispensed with bedding and clothes altogether, the elderly and the very young keeping each other company, avoiding bedsores and rashes and sleeping in hammocks that swung mesmerically over the quelling pond. The elderly were rocking the young to sleep and the young exhausting the elderly to the point where they could only look forward to their afternoon nap. (Hot metal pipes curled like sea serpents in the four corners of the room, well away from tiny curious hands.)

I began to fall asleep in this dormitory along with many others (it was overheated, I decided), but Marie-Victoire pinched me awake and took me down to the bowels of the almshospital where a giant furnace spat and raged.

Here a young man wearing practically nothing fuelled coal into a cauldron, constantly stopping to wipe the sweat from his brow. Every now and then the furnace gave off a mighty explosion and this scantly-clad descendant of Vulcan would leap back in fright, curse the fire and suck on his blistering burns.

Down the corridor from the furnace was a steam room (designed to heal those with respiratory infections) and three male attendants stood up when Marie-Victoire knocked at the foggy glass door. They gestured to us to enter but the steam was so hot and overpowering I refused. The men were standing in the swirls of cloud, their hair sticking to their foreheads, their linen shirts and trousers almost peeling off them in the dampness. There was something about the trio and the way they stood and the secrets their faces shared which reminded me of paintings of the three Graces I'd seen in the Ursuline convent. There was a similarity in the way the men looked, yet they were probably not even related. There was a symmetry about the way they stood, statue-proud though fluid in their movements, never moving out of the frame of the doorway that held them in its rectangular arms. It was as if they were three blooms sprung out of the same flower stalk. This was odd because I don't remember seeing men joined at the seams this way before, becoming themselves in the same poised sequence of actions.

They were male Graces, I decided, and they were always there in the steam room in the mornings when I came to pick up the steam-pressed bed linen, which had been washed in the river the day before, to take upstairs to the indisposed and forlorn. They were a single candelabra bearing three candlesticks and there was beauty in their closeness and the strength of arms they enfolded around each other as they bathed Roman-style in the steam. Even if it was no more than a skin-deep intimacy, a higher aesthetic had yoked these young men together and I wished that someone would come and paint the male Graces for me so that I could look at them in the privacy of my home again and again.

One morning when I looked in on the steam room, the male Graces were holding a newborn baby in their arms. They were passing it to each other and fondling it as though it was their own. I don't know where that baby came from because they didn't let babies be born in the almshospital with all the sick people around. This baby was naked and it seemed contented to be in the steam room with the male Graces, and the men seemed to love it even though it could not possibly be their own. (It couldn't belong to all three of them, could it?) That was the only baby I ever saw in the almshospital and it was only that one time. I kept thinking about it though and wondering where it had come from and what became of it. I continued to gaze in on the male Graces in wistful admiration. (After that first day and the obligatory introductions they completely ignored me and no conversation ever sprung up between us.)

Emerging back into the world of air after my days spent in the almshospital my ears would pop and water would run out of them — enough to fill a cup from each ear, which was a curious thing for I'd never supposed I had so much water in me. I would go home to my mother and she would marvel that my clothes were fresh and dry as if they'd just been steam-cleaned and ironed. I had no explanation for this except to tell her that my two worlds did not seem to connect. I was either saturated or completely dry.

I told made-up stories to the invalids all day. I read newspapers and even revolutionary pamphlets. I'd read anything to keep them entertained, while my thoughts were clicking away privately in my head like a pair of knitting needles. Sometimes I'd wonder about the fate of my Carmelite sisters. They'd left France apparently, to join a religious order in Genoa. Memories of Giselle and Emmanuel also predominated. These mental sores festered away and on certain days I could hardly concentrate on anything else. Reading to the invalids my voice wore out like a wooden wheel which buckled and rolled awkwardly along as I continued to read page after soaking page with the waters up to my waist and rising. My Arab turban revolved and came loose as invalid children tugged and tugged on its frivolous ends, and my bodily trembles had begun to get on the nerves of Marie-Victoire.

As a cure she sent me diving down to pick up various odds and ends she required from the bottom of the ground floor aquarium. Once she wanted an old kettle with a broken spout to put some flowers in. Another time she sent me searching for pieces of a Grecian vase she was hoping to cement back together and sit on her cherry commode.

I would swim down the way I'd done as a child, breaststroking to the bottom of the Rhône to find the tuning fork my father had thrown down there for us to fetch. I collected dozens of coins which when dried and placed on a tablecloth upstairs turned out to be large gold buttons, not coins at all. In fact every button lost to the world seemed to have found its way to the floor of the old street-level dormitory. My pockets bulged with more and more each time I resurfaced.

I pocketed button after button as though they really were the jewels they appeared to be when looking down at them twinkling below. In a fit of excitement I decided I would leave the almshospital and open a button shop, for I had so many buttons in perfect condition, including the ones that shone like florins, the ones which certainly must have been shed from the greatcoats of army officers, and also the tiny mother-of-pearl ones from women's evening gloves. In the afternoons I would take my tin of buttons and go from invalid to invalid shaking it in their faces while searching for missing buttons on their clothing, sewing on new ones whether they needed them or not. I could talk anyone into taking buttons from me, for if I wasn't sewing buttons on clothes or diving down to find new ones I quickly became dissatisfied. Among the little children on the upper floor I made immediate friends for they felt the same way about buttons as I did. My own clothes were now festooned with buttons (more button than cloth, some complained). When I walked into the dormitories some of the invalids would dive under their covers to avoid my ever-invasive needle and thread.

So preoccupied was I by my button collecting that I quite forgot I had a tremoring affliction, until the day my eyes met a trio of duckshooters (guns cocked) on the other side of the window when I was diving down to collect my treasure. A trio of duckshooters and moving in for the kill. Oh Marie-Victoire, Marie-Victoire, our ducks! The ducks we sheltered were at great risk and there was much flustering round the flustered ducks but we saved them all, except for a silly one that sailed out an open window and landed with a splash in the canal where we could offer it no protection.

The tremoring returned. I kept expecting the duckshooters to return and aim their guns at me. 'But you're wearing your button-plated vest!' protested Marie-Victoire. Thinking I was losing contact with reality, she sent me out of the almshospital for some daily exercise. Every afternoon, instead of reading aloud to the patients and buttonholing them for buttons, I walked down to the Rhône with a bar of soap in my pocket and a basket of soiled linen on my hip. It was the thought of this walk and its blessing of private and public solitude (it was both work and escape from work) that kept my spirits high in the following months when my bodily affliction was beginning to wear me down.

I was happiest in those few minutes walking to and from the river attended by stray cats and the odd glassy-eyed fisherman. Fishermen, I noticed, always have eyes like fish. I was childless but I had my bundle of linen and oilskins nonetheless. My face in the water was reassuring to me, as reassuring as the face of my mother appearing in an unexpected place. I became the washing-in-the-Rhône maiden and a local painter captured me at my post kneeling on a glittering carpet of fish scales with the water sliding up my elbows like a pair of black gloves and my apron-of-Avignon billowing around me in the breeze.

Some of the people who bought these watercolours in the Place de L'Horloge actually came walking round the riverbend to see if I really existed. Every afternoon at two o'clock I could be seen dunking my sheets in the river, stretching them out and pulling them in like nets, and now I had a little audience of aspiring watercolourists mythologising my labours, for the attention of one painter had inspired others and they were setting up easels around me so that I could no longer wash in peace.

At about this time a female domestic came up to me in the almshospital and offered me a button for my thoughts. I accepted the gilt button she held out and, turning it both ways, could tell her what year the button had been designed and in which workshop it had been made. I searched my tin and found another exactly like it, offering to give them both back to her in exchange for a *rose* Pompadour button that was fastening the nape of her blouse. I had recognised this button as a rare one, and when it came into my possession I found the mark of the famous porcelain factory in Vincennes-Sèvres on the other side.

The domestic agreed to the exchange but said I still had to tell her my thoughts. I told her about the watercolourists on the riverbank and how they were annoying me (I did not tell her about Emmanuel and Giselle whom I'd most likely been thinking about since they were rarely absent from my mind), and she said she would wash linen with me the following afternoon.

Violette was her name. She told me that first day we swapped buttons she had a too-trusting nature but she couldn't give it up because it was her own. Nonetheless she had been quite happy to change her name in a debaptism ceremony from 'boring old Marie-Anne'. Violette had hair the colour of violet ink and very impressive maternal breasts. She was sensual in body and deed and liked to touch the flanks of buildings as we walked along the narrow paths to the water lanes. She would hold up her chalky palms to me with delight. She could smell perfumes in the air and name them: cloves, thyme or tangerine orange. I had vaguely imagined scents to be there but could hardly distinguish one from another.

When I first met Violette there was a simplicity between us; we knew we liked each other but we hardly knew why. So different from me, she had grown up in a family of women and she had never even thought about being a nun.

I was more romantic than her, yet knowledge ruled me. It sent me off on explorative quests, refused to let me repeat myself in exactly the same way, defeated me time and time again, but never deserted me. (Knowledge was as ever-nourishing as *casserole de mouton*.)

Each of Violette's senses had developed like an opening rose. I let my senses ruffle wisdom or I liked to think I did, but wisdom never let them in the front door. They blew around outside, frustrated, alternatively bullying or seductive. After all, romance is born of the brain. It is not a thing of the body.

Violette let wisdom temper her senses. She had a more balanced constitution than me. Life had injured her (she'd lost her father when she was ten, her favourite sister when she was twenty) but it had also defined her more closely. Frailer on the surface I was in reality the more determined. Violette had more self-awareness. She had never denied herself close intimacies with others. Even with men. Especially with men, she said, wanting to impress me and naturally doing so. Violette told me I needed to get to know some real men myself. Not the male Graces. Not imaginary cousins. I scoffed and said I already knew about men because I had three brothers. I had no illusions. Violette said I had to forget my brothers and start again.

The local watercolourist (whose name was Joseph) and his imitators now painted Violette and myself as we washed on the banks of the Rhône. Violette claimed it was unfair that we should be subjected to this scrutiny when we were trying to clean dirty clothing. As if it wasn't undignified enough to be labouring over a brew of muddy Rhône and foul linen. She very politely informed the artists they should give us a commission on any work they sold.

The painter (the initial painter that is, the only one with any skill or talent) said he was really only interested in capturing the troubadour song of the river as it coursed past us on its scenic route south. We kneeling, biblical women were a necessary sideshow in his painting, a human anchoring, if we understood what he meant. The river with its legendary secrets and dancing lights was far more important to him than we were. It wasn't his fault we had chosen to wash in this little promontory where purple-grey Mount Ventoux could be viewed as a burgeoning storm cloud in the background.

After work Violette and I would sometimes meander round the walls of our town then cut through the more established streets to the place of the clocks where Joseph's pictures were for sale, often still drying in the sunshine, unframed but pegged to wooden slats lain across the cobblestones to trip up passers-by and make them look and then perhaps want to buy.

Some townspeople would pay to see these river pastorals decorating their bedroom walls, fading behind glass as the years progressed. Violette and I would live on, perhaps a hundred years from now, looking more and more like grubby sheep quenching our thirst at a cerulean carpet of river. *Rhône-maidens of Avignon* the painter Joseph had scratched into the corner of some of his paintings even though we looked nothing like our real selves. As we stared at the stiffening paper with its delicate stains, Violette and I could apprehend how humble was our occupation yet how graceful that waterbird swoop Joseph had given us.

Having seen myself immortalised as a Rhône-maiden I didn't want to be one any more. I would wash linen for fifty more days and that would be it. Having seen herself portrayed as a Rhône-maiden, Violette grew dissatisfied with the paintings themselves and demanded in a hurt and tremulous little voice that the painter conceal their more obvious flaws. Her own image was unflattering. No-one would recognise this hunched figure merging with the water as herself. Joseph was amused by my friend's tearful protests and surprisingly undefensive. They both seemed to be enjoying the altercation, for a moment later something Joseph said, which I did not catch, transformed her tears into smiles.

I bought one of the watercolours for Violette (the only one that made her look a little like a woman and not a bird or sheep) and I paid with my stipend savings, an action which made me feel resilient, as if I'd taken a swig from a bottle of whisky. I took Violette home and showed her Emmanuel's violin, one of my most prized possessions. (It had never been the same after the mistral incident and he had reluctantly given it to me.) I could still hear my cousin's voice in the twang of the strings. I could hear the mistral blowing through the wood if I held it up to my ear.

Violette crawled under my spinet while I played a Haydn minuet for her. She lay on her back and listened to the muffled sound. She played with the pedals at my feet like a small child. I remembered Giselle, but Violette was gentler than Giselle. She was older and with so many sisters she'd had to learn how to share. I already sensed she and Joseph were going to be lovers but I didn't mind this time. Although life doesn't always give you what you want, it hardly ever serves you up the same dish twice. I wasn't jealous of Joseph. I liked him as much as my almshospital friend. He deserved her affection.

Violette's mother sewed me a dress the colour of grass. She embroidered the hem with a band of red cotton. Joseph began to paint me in the dress, sitting at my spinet. He told me to stop trembling and I was so much in awe of him I did manage to do as he asked, but I got the hiccups instead. He made Violette rub my back and he distracted us with funny stories about the aristocrats he'd painted and how he frequently had sneezing fits on entering their grand old homes because of the excesses of perfumes and powders they used to hide the stench of their unwashed bodies. Joseph was painting me and Violette was sitting next to me on the spinet stool, drawing Joseph at his easel with a wry smile on her face. (She never let Joseph see these drawings. There was obviously some titillation for her in both the drawing and the subsequent withholding.)

I went swimming in the Rhône in my new dress, which is mostly how people in Avignon clean their clothes, if they bother at all. The fabric had been made in a foreign place and the dark green dye came out of it, much to my dismay and the dismay of those swimming near me whose clothes ended up the same pale green as mine.

Joseph was keen to finish my portrait so he made me wear the faded fresco-green dress for the sittings and smothered it with dark green paint. This experience (of him painting the dress while I was wearing it) made my skin tingle. My cheeks and the base of my neck grew flushed. Previously Joseph had painted my actual face with a carmine-tipped brush to give it a rosy glow. Now he said he didn't need to bother.

I sat at my spinet smelling of oils, listening to the banter between the painter and my friend. A warm current flowed between them and I was grateful they did not exclude me from its midst. I was making up for lost time, though people say you can never really do that in life. If I was making up for years spent in a convent, then in the future I would be nurturing children like everyone else my age seemed to be doing. I would be forever playing a game of catch-up. Perhaps I would keep trying to make an entry into the world and failing because everyone else had moved on ahead.

No-one had neglected me. I had neglected myself. Here I was, a displaced former nun wondering whom to trust and what to believe when there was no-one to trust (apart from one's closest kin) and very little one might confidently believe in. I suspected the only way of restoring my childhood was to have children of my own, yet marriage to anyone but Emmanuel (he to whom I'd been betrothed in all but word and deed, despite my lingering doubts) would be like short-changing myself and everything in me that still needed some sort of God to believe in. In the absence of the Catholic Trinity (whom we were not allowed to believe in any more) and in the absence of the real Emmanuel, I could only believe in my cousin more fervently than ever.

In the compensatory Giselle-like afternoons I spent with Violette, I swam along the pleasurable surface of life, caught within one of Monsieur Joseph's spangled watercolours of the river. In Violette's company there always reverberated that memory of the channel I had once been rowing down with Emmanuel. In Violette's presence I felt his absence most persistently. My love for my cousin, though imaginary, was as true as it was untrue. We were connected by family ties, joined by those differences which keep royalist and republican locked in perpetual debate. Held apart and soldered together by a rhetoric of love and hate.

All roads led to Emmanuel, and all canals and watercolours too.

By the time Joseph finished his portrait of me in a green dress at my spinet I had watched the feeling between him and Violette develop from something tenuous and uncertain into something obvious and secure. I had seen them navigate each other, explore and tempt each other, yet never lose control in a subtle exchange of feeling which unfolded before my shyly observing eyes. They would move a little closer for affection, then draw back feigning disinterest, then move a little closer again, like a game of cat and mouse.

There was never any expression of cruelty or contempt because they weren't particularly scared of each other. They knew they were on the same side now and they were relaxing a little. Violette continued to make unsolicited drawings of Joseph, exaggerating the muscles in his thighs and colouring in his shirts to amuse herself, but he adamantly refused to do a formal portrait of her. By the edge of the river yes, with her back to him he was happy to paint her as a swan (she had such an inspiring behind, he told her very rudely), and he was there every afternoon at the riverbend with a dwindling circle of followers imitating his style, their easels staked out around him at different levels on the slope.

I couldn't help noticing that this was an alliance of feelings conducted so differently from that which took place between Giselle and Philippe, who had latched onto each other so furiously, forgetting the rest of the world and me especially.

Violette and Joseph could exist without each other and they could exist with me in the middle, nestling between them, rubbing shoulders as we strolled along Avignon laneways and streets. I usually accompanied them on picnics to the countryside on our days off from the almshospital. They insisted I join them, perhaps because they felt more comfortable with someone else deflecting their attention from each other. They seemed happy for their relationship to remain as chaste and casual as possible.

I was keen to learn the language of love wherever it was on offer because I was about as ignorant as Robinson Crusoe on the subject. I always accepted their invitations enthusiastically, knowing they would never make me feel as if I was tagging along.

On one of our excursions to the sparsely populated islands of the Rhône we lay side to side in the dry grass and Joseph told stories about the three years he'd spent in the navy as a very young man. He told us how the vain admirals kept thinking they'd discovered new continents which turned out to be small uninhabitable islands with a shipwrecked sailor or two they would have to take on board whether they had room for them or not. He recalled with delight that the sailors had fished all day and got drunk every night, in which state they'd cursed the English and Dutch for passing them with their better-made ships.

The painter told us these stories and made us laugh and our response seemed to please him as much as telling the stories did. Lying on my back between Joseph and Violette and looking at the sky I could see the sun at one o'clock browning the fruit on a nearby thorn apple tree. Lying on my back I could see the web of leaves and branches revealing clusters of small hard fruit and I could also see a pair of human feet and ankles dangling down from the bottommost wreath of leaves.

'Violette,' I said seriously, 'someone is caught in the tree.'

I got up and took five steps quickly forwards then five steps slowly backwards.

A young man wearing a surplice and cassock was hanging from a branch, swinging gently in the breeze with a rope around his neck.

None of us had expected to encounter such a gruesome spectacle so far from the centre of hostilities. Joseph recognised the priest but he didn't know his name. Recovering from the unpleasant surprise, he climbed the tree and began to cut the rope with a bread knife from our picnic basket. Violette and I followed his instructions as though in a trance. We held the priest by the legs and bore his weight when the knife cut through the rope. Then we slowly lowered him to the ground and laid him on his back.

The priest's eyes were closed, his feet were bare and there were thorn apples sticking to his hair and clothes. The painter jumped down from the tree and began pulling the thorn apples out, one by one, enlisting us to help.

'What shall we do with him?' I asked, feeling like my spirit had departed my body and was floating away as fast as it could.

'Bury him of course,' Joseph answered bluntly.

Violette burst into tears and because neither of us was able to comfort her she ran off into the woods.

The painter told me to go and get her for he'd need our help to bury the priest quickly. If we were discovered doing so we might be accused of assisting an enemy of the republic.

When she returned, still sobbing, Joseph lost his temper with her. He shook her violently, which so startled her she stopped crying straightaway. Joseph told her she'd better keep her wits about her or we might also be strung up from the same tree by nightfall. What's more he had no intention of betrothing himself to someone who couldn't deal with the unexpected in a calm and considerate manner.

His words were so sharp I put my arm around Violette. I urged Joseph to get on with the matter in hand. I did not like to ask him how this burying could be done in case he thought it another foolish question he could well do without. Though it took several hours and much energy and inventiveness, we succeeded in marking out a burial place in the woods, well away from the tree where roaming brigands might come looking for the body with the intention of mutilating it.

Violette and Joseph called upon me as a former religious sister to bless the dead man. This invitation came as a surprise because I knew from a theological discussion we'd had earlier in the day that Violette was a deist and Joseph had no faith other than a belief in a combined god who represented work and aesthetic beauty. Yet we'd all been brought up in the Catholic faith.

I made a crude crucifix twisting two sticks together with a grapevine, and just before we lowered the young priest into the ground I said a requiescat in pace which I knew off by heart from my convent years. I spoke the words and they seemed more meaningful than any I'd uttered in my whole life.

When the priest lay a few feet under soil and we had put our digging sticks aside, we were overwhelmed with a sense of relief. Now I understood why Joseph had felt it necessary to religiously fulfil this task which was against both our normal jurisdictional law as well as the revolutionary dictates currently being enforced by the local authorities. (No-one was allowed to secretly bury the dead and Catholic ceremonies had been outlawed by the Jacobin Convention the previous year.) The young priest was dead and we could do nothing about that, but at least he was resting in peace. We could leave him without feeling guilty because we had buried him with dignity.

Afterwards we hurried from the place, returning to the town by an indirect route which Joseph said would help cover our tracks in the event of an investigation into the priest's whereabouts. We were to tell everyone we'd spent the afternoon in Villeneuve with Violette's aunt, a gentlewoman we briefly visited that evening. Joseph said there was no need for honesty in a situation like this.

He had removed a handkerchief and a house key from the priest's pockets and wanted to return these personal belongings to the dead man's family wherever they were living. He said he was going to write a note (in copperplate rather than in longhand to protect his identity in case the note fell into the hands of the revolutionary guards) explaining exactly where the priest was buried so that his family would know where to find him.

Joseph wrapped the key in the handkerchief and gave it to me to hide in my house. He knew I would be able to keep quiet if necessary. I said goodbye to my friends in the darkness, thinking very selfishly that I would definitely let them picnic on their own in future.

In the morning, returning to work, I told Marie-Victoire I'd had enough washing linen in the Rhône. I was going diving in the afternoons once more and she could make a list of things she wanted from the bottom of the ground-floor aquarium. Marie-Victoire considered me doubtfully. Then she asked me if I knew my face had contracted. Looking at my reflection in the almshospital waters I noticed my face was indeed thinner than it had been before: I was looking older.

As I dived down into the waters that afternoon I was determined to reclaim the joy such diversion had given me in the past, but I was only deceiving myself in thinking I could go back to that sanctuary of sweet delirium. The fluid enveloping my skin felt cold and unaccommodating. My eyes stung when I opened them and my ears ached when they filled with liquid.

The underwater room had lost its magic potency. Nothing exciting was waiting to be discovered among the debris on the floor. Everything I picked up looked well worth throwing away. (Does escape cease to be profitable when one recognises it as such?)

I knew what I was doing this time. I knew I was trying to cut myself free of the tenuous threads binding me to Joseph and Violette. If I had not let myself get attached to them in the first place I would not have the memory of the priest which now needed to be erased from my mind so I could get on with my life.

Later that evening, in my attic room, I opened the white handkerchief Joseph had entrusted me with and took out the dead priest's house key. It rested coldly in my hand. Made of a hardy metal but curiously unmarked by the passage of life. I wondered if this virgin key had ever turned in a lock before. (Perhaps reading house keys is like reading palms and this unlined key already told of its master's death.)

I might get up in the night and walk from house to house and open three thousand doors before I found the door this key would open. And I wouldn't know till the key turned in the lock that it was the right door. I might enter and encounter a family who vaguely resembled the young priest. They would look at me in surprise then hate me for the news I brought them. They would always remember me, not as a brave and truthful messenger, but as a black-hooded executioner of the heart.

I stared at the key that would open a door but not the right person that owned the key whom I would liked to have met alive. That young priest would always be an absent figure to me now.

He had carried this key. It had rested between his fingers and perhaps in one of his pockets and now it was resting between mine but he was never going to know that. In a year or two (if fate had chanced otherwise) I might have gone into his church and taken the sacrament from him. I might have contemplated a caring face that now I was only ever going to be able to imagine dead.

What kind of initiation into the life of another is it to be a witness at their death? As intimate as if you had been a witness at their birth. (And as unforgettable.)

I scented the young priest's handkerchief with frangipane to ward off the spirits of the dead, then I dried my eyes with it. It was soft and worn (unlike the key) and I was going to ask the painter if I could keep it.

I didn't want to see Violette and Joseph together again but I knew I was going to have to. They made me feel vulnerable and somehow implicated in their engagement. I almost felt as though they were waiting for me to give them the signal to become one. (Maybe Joseph and Violette would even call upon me to marry them as a high priestess of France's new Goddess of Reason religion.)

I chided myself for getting tangled up in other people's lives.

'It is possible,' said Papa, coming in to say goodnight and sensing my distress, 'it is possible to ford daunting looking streams in life and come out safely on the other side.'

'Mama wouldn't agree with you,' I answered defensively. 'She'd say keep on walking and you might find a bridge.'

Then a memory of childhood came back, of Noah's Flood, as it was always referred to. My father was away in Arles when disaster struck our town and swept so many away as they stood in their doorways and watched. We were poorer and living in a wooden cottage next to a dairy. When Mama saw the first of the battered barges come careering down our road she and I climbed the sturdy plum tree behind our cottage, carrying the younger boys with us. We sat there in the rain watching the waters enter our humble house. Mama was trying to make the best of our loss (wooden cottages capsizing around us like fishing boats) with Emile suckling at her breast and me eating plums (a rope joining me to Constantine by the waist in case he fell). We saw houses floating past with people sitting on the rooftops. We saw children riding logs of wood, screaming for their mamas, screaming for their papas, as the swiftly flowing current rushed them by.

The waters rose up the trunk of our tree then slowly receded. I watched, oblivious to any danger in this fanciful world with my mother close by, sheltered from the brunt of the rain by the tree's awning of leaves.

My adult self recalls the tree had stood in the place where a drinking well later came to be. My father cut down the plum tree and dug a well where the roots grew, and because of this the water always tasted sweeter than normal and sometimes (in summer) quite distinctly of plums.

As I closed my eyes remembering our first home and that old plum tree with its purple leaves which used to rustle like a woman's starched petticoat in the breeze, I fell asleep wishing I could return to the warm nest of my mother's love. And be forever five.

6

The bridge
of Avignon

*T*here is an imaginary bridge in the mind of those born in Avignon. A bridge that stretches from one side of the river to the other and doesn't end in the middle. The full-length bridge should exist, it certainly could if we wanted it too, but we don't really want it to any more. Forty years ago it existed. Seven handspans across it was. 'Seven cartwheels to the other side and seven stone fans back' goes the clapping song we used to sing, raising our arms (in pairs) then collapsing our bridges again and again.

In the compression of her arches her strength and stability lie. From the riot of our seasonal floods her wreck and ruin stem. Now we no longer think of our neighbours in Villeneuve as part of ourselves.

Fantasies thicken and consume. The more the fantasy blooms the less chance the two ends have of meeting in the middle. Children of Avignon grow up making toy bridges in their homes and designing bridges in their schools and going to Paris (city of plentiful *ponts*) in their imaginations. Avignon people are funny about bridges, so say visitors to this town. Bridge fever is an illness similar to that which amputees get when they think they can walk on their severed limb. Sleepwalkers are attracted to the bridge and many have awoken from their slumber attempting to cross in their nightshirts upon the olden-day bridge that haunts our dreams.

We look embarrassed and change the topic when strangers question us about the Pont Saint Bénézet (it is our secret failing, our Achilles heel), yet all round the town are signs we believe in bridges with an architect's faith. Puddles have skipping ropes thrown over them as soon as they appear in the backstreets and lanes. Wooden walkways crisscross the canals. You can walk on raised slats through the perfume fountains in the gardens of Castle Rock, then dry your flower-scented clothes in the sun. Many do this, especially those who can't afford toilet water in their homes.

There are bridges in the air. Chimneys are connected by mistletoe at Noël and acquaintances greet each other by reaching out and touching shoulders with their hands. Right hand of the first onto the shoulder of the second and vice versa.

In medieval times when the pope lived amongst us, a narrow bridge with twenty-two little arches spanned the Rhône and people thought it was held up by angels. Horses and farm animals crossed all day in a steady stream. Peasants took their lives into their hands each time they set out from one side of town to the other.

There is a thirteenth-century fresco of the bridge in our cathedral and you can see people crossing in blindfolds, their swords held up protectively in front of them as though they expected to meet with disaster at any time. They had porters to help the nervous and frail across. In the fresco you can see these porters holding the blindfolded by the arms and urging on the sheep and goats with sticks.

As a young girl I could never work out why the scared wore blindfolds when they were crossing. Wouldn't that make them more scared, not being able to see? The Ursuline sister who taught us religious art said they wore blindfolds so they could pretend they weren't walking over a swiftly flowing river. They could imagine they were still on firm ground.

In the religious fresco the bridge-crossers weren't all scared. Some had their eyes open wide and were looking at the river with much curiosity, but the painter had made these ones look a little dazed and foolhardy. A young man in a brown hood was vomiting over the side of the railings. He'd obviously seen far too much light in a short space of time. You felt the ones with the blindfolds on had the right attitude for that day and age.

Every year of my life for as long as I can remember there'd be discussions at mealtimes about rebuilding the bridge and how much money it would cost, but nothing happened because people had grown used to living without one. We were attached to our broken bridge in the same way parents can become more attached to a lame child than to their other children.

Because the Pont Saint Bénézet was now little more than a pier to which barges and boats were daily tethered, it became a place frequented by those wishing for restrained activity in a breezy setting. Children conglomerated on the bridge in the arms of their nurses or unattended in small bunches to play at the edges of care.

Lovers invariably conducted the early phase of their romance upon this open-air promenade and it was here that Violette, growing sick of Joseph's refusal to paint her properly (she wanted him to use oils and paint her supine on an ottoman sofa), pushed him fully dressed into the Rhône while he was trying to paint another couple strolling arm in arm along the bridge.

Though I did not see the incident, I heard about it from Violette. It was an action she regretted because Joseph had disappeared under the bridge and for ten dreadful minutes she thought he had drowned. He reappeared further down the riverbank and, seeing him, she ran over and embraced him. He pushed her away and walked off in his dripping cape, his paintbrushes (which he'd never let go of) held up like a bouquet in his hands. Violette didn't know if he had got into real difficulty or had just been pretending, but either way it looked less likely than ever she was going to have her portrait painted by him.

Though I had decided after the dead priest picnic to relinquish Joseph and Violette from my life, it turned out they had no intention of relinquishing me from theirs. Violette insisted we continue washing linen in the Rhône for she said it was her favourite hour of the day. She so persuasively convinced me of her genuine attachment I didn't have the heart to turn away from her.

I could not escape seeing her in the almshospital and after two weeks the spectre of the dead priest weakened and I ceased to associate Violette with his death and the pain this had caused me. In the evenings she would wait for me after work and accompany me to the marketplace or walk me to my door. I think she must have known desertion was on my mind for she assured me I meant as much to her as Joseph did. She would devote her entire evening to my company, encouraging me to teach her the flute and staying to share our evening meal of white cod and blanched thistle stems.

Our mothers didn't like us walking around the town when darkness had fallen, for sometimes there would be an eruption of hostilities between supporters of the new regime and supporters of the old. Violette was *for* the revolution and I was *against* the revolution, but neither of us knew what would be better for our country as a whole. Unsurprisingly we were more interested in our own concerns and spent hours discussing cures for my shaking illness and ways of getting Joseph to marry Violette.

The bloody strife was continuing in Paris but we in Avignon tried to lead quiet simple lives pretending the conflict belonged to someone else. Nevertheless, confusion hung like a cloud over our customary southern frivolity for we were unsure what was going to happen from one day to the next. People kept forgetting which day of the week it was. Many indeed refused to honour the ten-day working week, finding the idea of selling and sowing on the day which used to be Sunday repugnant to both body and soul.

The street names kept changing with the enthronement and deposition of Parisian leaders. One week you were walking along Rue de Lafayette and the next week it had become the Rue Marat. Some churches were allowed to open for recreational purposes but others remained closed with entry strictly forbidden. There seemed to be no particular logic as to why one church should become an arsenal and another a Temple of Reason. There seemed to be no particular logic about a lot of things.

In the streets peasants were seen dressed as kings (after robbing the houses of the rich) and nobles went around in rags, having perfected the art of dignified begging. Extremely beautiful women dressed as men (to avoid being raped), and men with a price on their heads dressed as pregnant women. Indeed any women who wanted a little more protection in our troubled times bound pillows to their waists and walked with a backward tilt, for only pregnant women were left alone, no matter what they had done, no matter what anyone said they had done.

There were so many women with big bellies parading through our town that a visiting Spanish dignitary wanted to know where all the infants born out of this plague of pregnancy happened to be hiding. Confinement as a fashion came into vogue and seamstresses made gowns that tucked in under the bosom then bulged significantly in that place of supposed growing (where padding had been discreetly sewn). Mime artists gave lessons on how to walk with convincing lower back pain and waddle like women in their final weeks of pregnancy. People got carried away and young women paid dozens of *Louis d'ors* to be seen in one of these vainglorious gowns.

At first everyone was saying how ungainly the outfits were and Violette told me she wouldn't be seen dead wearing one. Then we got used to the new dress style ('blossoming bellies' a Parisian fashion designer nicknamed them) and although we didn't yet find them attractive we stopped finding them unattractive. Before long Violette and I succumbed to the prevailing trend and our mothers set to work with needle and thread, Violette's mother making my gown and my own mama stitching away at Violette's so we wouldn't go fault-finding when the dresses were done.

When we went washing in the Rhône in our blossoming bellies Joseph would patronisingly offer us an arm as we sidled down onto our knees. He teased us mercilessly about the state of unmarried grace we found ourselves in. People could no longer distinguish the fashion from the real thing and women began to enjoy the mystery pertaining to their newly designated figures. There was a freedom in wearing a pregnancy gown which reminded me of how I felt when I was wearing my religious habit. Men would not touch us; they mostly refrained from even looking at us except to look away.

Blossoming bellies increased in size as the fashion spread like an infectious disease, and the six-month belly was soon replaced by the more desirable nine-month belly. As if this wasn't enough, the full-term belly was supplanted by the improbable overdue belly as dressmakers outdid each other to be first in their windows with a novel look.

In the almshospital I looked in through the steam room door one day and saw the male Graces wearing blossoming bellies completely unself-consciously. They were standing in a traditional fifteenth-century pose, their hands held out over their midriffs like dancers' hands. I couldn't make up my mind whether they were mocking us or copying us. I thought they looked beautiful in their lacy confinement clothes whether they were genuine about it or not, but Marie-Victoire, in one of her grumpy moods, was not impressed.

She told me they'd gone down considerably in her estimation for she could no longer respect them. 'Ridiculous, quite ridiculous,' she fumed. 'They're men, after all. They're supposed to be men, Marie-France.'

Yes. I could see they were still men. And I could tell by the expression on their faces they knew they were still men.

(They had lost none of their power over me.)

Thinking about the male Graces and what they had become kept me elated all day.

It was about this time that a small boy with consumption drowned in the almshospital. No invalid had drowned in the twenty-year history of our underwater institution.

The blossoming bellies were blamed for the tragedy. It was thought the domestics could no longer see clearly in front of them and hadn't noticed the sinking boy. This may have been the case for the gowns did obstruct our view. Marie-Victoire's feud with the steam room Graces may also have contributed, for she had recently neglected her normally vigilant observation of the dormitories.

She blamed herself for the loss of the child. (She told me she did.)

At pains to ensure it would never happen again, she harangued the local authorities to drain the almshospital of its medicinal fluids. They reluctantly agreed. Reluctantly because the people of our town had the same affection for our underwater almshospital as they did for our broken bridge. The authorities predicted that emotional scenes would occur and they were right.

A small crowd collected outside the almshospital and observed through the windows as the water level dropped. They told each other it was all for the best and they accepted what was taking place without too much resistance. (They still believed in the almshospital though. At some deeper level of understanding the waters had yet to recede from view.)

When the almshospital was drained we expected the canal it is built upon to flood, and the people whose houses abutted the building moved elsewhere for a week. When they returned nothing had happened to their homes.

Afterwards Violette and I went back inside the building to have a look. (The almshospital wasn't due to reopen officially for several months.) Shimmering illusions of water swirled and eddied around us. We moved slowly through the rooms, gracefully and buoyantly. It did not feel as if anything had changed. A week after the draining our townsfolk began to cry. Wherever you looked people were mopping tears from their eyes. Crying for no reason. The street sweepers, the bakers, the dandies and the old ladies wrapped in black — all becoming veritable *misérables*. Children, faces brimming with smiles, would leap off their chalk squares to wipe tears (instead of the usual snotty noses) on cuffs and sleeves.

Few of us knew why we were crying. The water had to come out somewhere and it came out in ourselves.

Violette and I continued to spend our evenings together and it was on our regular boat trips to visit her aunt in Villeneuve that we began to see Marie-Victoire standing on cliffs and monuments overlooking the river.

We saw her high on the hill of Rocher de Dom, waving at someone or something in the direction of Mount Ventoux. We saw her on the balcony of the Petit-

Palace with a fishing reel in her hands. The line appeared to be suspended all the way across the river and was held by a dim figure standing on the opposite bank. Then we saw her standing at the very end of the Pont Saint Bénézet, counting her fingers and talking to herself.

Marie-Victoire had taken temporary leave from the almshospital after the sick boy drowned. 'That boy was going to die anyway,' I told her, but this made no difference to how she felt. When the almshospital reopened, with its freshly painted surfaces and dry stone floors, she was unwilling to return to work. Marie-Victoire was looking, I think, for some other means of overcoming a despair which was not just about the boy but part of her everyday unhappiness.

When she saw Violette and me disembarking, Marie-Victoire called us over. She drew from her pocket a map of a new bridge of Avignon which she had designed herself. She had received permission from the local authorities to secure a rope walkway from the end of the existing bridge to the shores of Villeneuve. The plans showed a swinging bridge that would be quite an effort for those less than agile to cross. It looked like a woven hand-stretch across the water. Marie-Victoire had drawn a stick figure of herself halfway across the netting. There was another stick figure (unidentifiable as man or woman) waiting to meet her on the other side.

'We will walk across the water,' she said sanctimoniously, her voice a falsetto's in the breeze.

Violette and I both nodded. We didn't want to upset her. Walking back to the centre of town, Violette told me that Marie-Victoire's madness was not having the grand idea, it was believing she could make it happen.

'Perhaps she will make it happen,' I suggested. My friend just shook her glossy head.

Possibly the idea of a swinging rope-bridge was nonsensical, but there was definitely purpose for Marie-Victoire in building the bridge. It was the challenge of construction which tantalised her most, we agreed. That is why Violette and I became involved. Neither of us would have done so if we had thought it would be a waste of time.

'It's not an easy thing to lose one's religious vocation,' I said to Violette. 'How would you like to be forced to deny your most fundamental beliefs?'

'You just need more fresh air and long walks, Marie-France,' said my friend a little unsympathetically. 'And have you noticed, before you shake you usually stutter? Just like stage fright.'

'I was thinking of Marie-Victoire, not myself,' I replied.

'I guess she'd been an Augustan sister for an awfully long time,' my friend politely admitted. Then she yawned.

The next morning when we arrived on the bridge a group of chamberpot gypsies were already unfurling a quantity of rope from the back of an old fruitcart. They had enlisted some of their relatives to help. Violette and I were the ones to row the first length of rope across the river, securing it to a pylon with the help of a circus strongman. A second, third and fourth length were hammered into place. Then the weaving began in earnest.

We laboured but it did not feel like hard work. It was October on the old calendar and Grape Harvest on the new. My favourite temperate month and we did not mind being outside all day, exposed to the sun and wind. Like riggers on a tall ship we clung to our ropes and prayed for cloud when there was sun and prayed for sun when there was cloud. The chamberpot gypsies squirmed past us, weaving with dextrous skill, coils of rope slung over their shoulders as though they were horse trainers.

Marie-Victoire patrolled beneath our labours in a little boat, poking a long pointed stick at poor stitching and helping us untangle knots. Her stick looked like an enormous embroidery needle for it had a very prominent fork at the end. Our turbans unravelled on the blowy bridge and flapped at our ears like frustrated sails. 'Rum-te-tum,' sang Violette, hanging almost upside down from the ropes and swinging from side to side, 'I can see-saw a former nun.'

Marie-Victoire got a pair of shears and cut our veils in half so we wouldn't come under any suspicion. (Nuns were still having their heads chopped off in Paris.) Our hair hung down below our veils, looking very odd. 'Half a veil, half a bridge, half a husband and half a league forward,' said Violette, stretching her hand out across the water as we'd seen Marie-Victoire do so often.

Joseph had his easel mounted at the end of the stone bridge and was documenting our endeavours, at a considerable distance this time.

'Half a husband?' I enquired, but Violette refused to divulge anything further on this matter.

From our lofty position we could see men and women dancing in the water, their bodies conversing beneath the sheer blue surface. As day progressed our shadows became Goliath size, darkening the waters and protecting the lovers from our gaze.

'The best place to give birth is in water,' Violette said, looking down at the swimmers. 'The baby will swim up to the surface and greet you.'

We both smiled at the thought.

One of her sisters, a midwife, was always telling stories of miracle births where there was no pain for the mother. Women giving birth while riding horses or running down a blazing street. The baby just dropping between their legs, taking them totally by surprise. The ones who give birth while moving are spared the agony of the cross.

'The Virgin gave birth quietly, in a stable,' I commented.

Violette nodded. 'Do you know what my sister has to say about that? She says that Mary must have been milking a cow. She would have been squatting down when her pains began. That's why they didn't hurt.'

After the construction of the rope-bridge had been underway for several weeks, the painter noticed something unusual about its design.

'It's going up not across, you realise, mademoiselles.'

We looked. Yes, we had noticed but we hadn't considered what this might mean. The webbing was rising far and above that which was necessary for the completion of the bridge. It had not looked like this in Marie-Victoire's plans. She was directing the gipsies to weave the mesh of ropes skywards rather than strengthening the bridge along the guy ropes, which would have made walking to the facing shore possible. Each day a little more of our skyline was obscured by her grid.

Marie-Victoire had left her boat and was situated at the highest point on the ropes. She was drawing inspiration from the sky rather than the Villeneuve wetlands. As we watched, the scaffolding of a church slowly came into view.

When Violette and I approached Marie-Victoire the next morning and asked her about the change of direction she showed us a new plan. Here was a steeple held aloft by nothing it would seem. The rope-bridge was merely holding up a threadbare cathedral. The stick figure representing Marie-Victoire was sketched high up on the ropes and the stick figure on the other riverbank had risen high in the sky too, but was no nearer to the first figure than before. Looking more closely with my eyeglasses on I could see that the stick figures were quite possibly both meant to represent Marie-Victoire. There was a voluminous gown on each of them and miniscule half-veils on their heads, though the second figure was drawn rather more hazily than the first and it was impossible to be completely sure about her (or perhaps even his) identity. The figure on the opposite bank was raised on a pillar of cloud.

Which way were we meant to weave then?

Marie-Victoire was no longer sure herself. She pointed both ways, up and across, telling us our destination was the opposite bank whereas hers was sitting in the clouds.

Violette and I got into a boat and rowed across the river. We sat on the Villeneuve bank and observed Marie-Victoire climbing the ropes to the point where it looked like they were attached to the sky. Held there by faith alone.

It happens when giving birth, Violette told me. The body straining in different directions. The desire to push before the womb is fully open. You must complete the first stage before you move on to the second. Otherwise it can be dangerous. You must not push the baby out until the neck of the womb is completely open.

I imagined wombs opening like giant clams and wondered if my own womb would ever be entirely open to another person as it would have to be if I were to have a child of my own. I pictured Marie-Victoire making her fatal crossing with a baby's head stuck inside a concave womb-neck.

'Stuck inside her brain more like it,' commented my uncharacteristically acerbic friend.

Impatience has no attendant virtues to recommend it. The ladder to heaven is rung along the corridor to hell so woe to he or she who slips and falls.

Alone at my writing desk I opened a Bible and followed Moses across the sea of reeds with the mighty sheets of water parted at either side. We walked across the dry ground and I had a purple halo hovering over my head. (It didn't belong to me.) When we reached the other side my halo spun off and the sea closed its shutters and returned to normal. Our palms and clothes were dry. We didn't have to wring them out. Our hearts burst open and blood shot out and watered the plants all around us and the frogs in the marshes choked to death.

Blood is not water. Sky is not God, nor can He make up for lack of human love.

On earth we can only rely on each other.

In the skies over Avignon Marie-Victoire was now as high as the Petit Palace. Her web was on the point of giving way to the imperatives of gravity. Dozens of children climbed the ropes to hold her hand. Some said she could cure illness at a touch. (Like a spider she removed herself from her tapestry in the darkness and went home to her humble lodgings every night.)

During the day townspeople conglomerated on the riverbanks and fortifications, expecting her to fall. Something had to change. She'd been weaving in the same position for a week, treading rope, sensing that if she climbed any higher the whole structure would collapse.

In sympathy, concerned families brought their own rope supplies along and attached these to the faltering bridge to lend it greater support. Soon hundreds of new ropes were tied to Marie-Victoire's bridge-tower by well-wishers intent on keeping her safely aloft. Lines of rope extended across our little city in a matter of days. Everyone wanted a connection running from their homes to the cathedral-on-Rhône. Violette and I could hardly walk around the town, so obstructed were we by the ropes angling down in all directions. Carriages could no longer go where they pleased, which was very annoying for drivers and passengers alike, but those on horseback simply jumped the ropes (if they were low enough) or led their animals underneath instead.

When Violette and I couldn't find Marie-Victoire in the sky one morning we knew something must have happened to her. Fishermen told stories of seeing her boarding a boat shortly after dawn, a boat that disappeared down the river in the direction of Arles. The full story unravelled bit by bit over a period of weeks.

Apparently a boatload of fishermen (irritated by her walkway's interference with the normal flow of river traffic) had invited her to share a meal with them in their village south of our town. One of the men, a widower, had treated Marie-Victoire with a special interest and she had responded favourably and found herself a new bed in his home in Barbentane. The bed was not a matrimonial bed at first, as she merely agreed to be his housekeeper, but it soon became so.

Once Marie-Victoire was ensconced in Barbentane the other fishermen wasted no time in showing how they wholeheartedly despised her creative efforts. The rope-bridge was withdrawn from view, skein by skein.

The men cut the rope into equal portions and departed excitedly with what they had each acquired. It was as though they were confiscating pirate booty!

One evening Avignon children were diving off the rope-bridge like flying fish, the next the entire tapestry had disappeared forever from our midst. In their homes townspeople pulled in the now slack offerings of support while barking dogs went wildly chasing the withdrawing ropes this way and that along the winding streets.

The December mistral would have brought the swinging bridge down if the fishermen hadn't. It would not have survived the season of frost in our city of violent winds, but I was disappointed with the outcome nonetheless. Marie-Victoire had not completed what she had set out to do.

Violette wasn't disappointed. She said the construction of the bridge was a bit like a play we'd all been acting in. We should be thankful the drama had ended happily and possible tragedy had been averted.

'I regret only that I'm too old to have a child,' Marie-Victoire confided to me when I bumped into her in the marketplace the following spring.

'The fishermen pulled down your bridge and took it all away,' I blurted out, but she did not share my dismay.

'Oh, you mean my peacock tail?'

I was puzzled.

'My husband says it was a great lure, that bridge. I was fanning my feathers with only one intention in mind.' Marie-Victoire was smiling at me but it was a dismissive smile, dismissive of me and of the past whose truth she was altering for her own peace of mind.

Like the rest of Avignon, Violette and I went back to rowing across the river in the ancient way. Our arms grew so strong our mothers had to slit the sleeves of our blossoming bellies and sew them up with velvet hearts.

They went on and on about how well we were looking. I'd have to agree concerning Violette. About myself I wasn't so sure.

Some days I forgot I had the trembling malady. Other times, when my nerves were on edge, Violette had to administer all the cinnamon syrup to the invalids because of the mess I made with mine. In the steam room (unchanged from the flooded almshospital days) the male Graces shuddered in unison as I passed their door. When I entered their abode to collect fresh linen they jostled each other like fishmongers. I took no offence for I did not realise their mimicry was aimed at me.

The charmers on the second floor wanted to put me to sleep along with those in considerable pain and I accepted their offer because Violette said it was worth a try. They covered me with poppies and swung their spells but their spells did not work, though I closed my eyes and prayed that they would. The charmers conferred on the matter and came to the conclusion that I had hypnotised myself. The bodily fugue which punctuated my days (a legacy of my time in the Avignon Academy of Dance) was itself a relief.

My condition, if anything, had worsened with Marie-Victoire's departure. There was no-one in a position of authority much of the time, and occasionally it was left to me to make administrative decisions. This was distressing because I was not used to taking responsibility for myself, let alone others. Though I knew I was not physically well, I remained optimistic that I would be restored to full health in the not too distant future. I kept reminding myself that the fever is at its peak just before the sick person turns the corner to recovery.

Violette and I continued washing linen in the Rhône and this daily respite from the almshospital (both work and escape from work) was still a pleasurable venture for each of us. It was in this place that Violette, bending forward on her hands and knees one afternoon, without any prior warning or announcement, gave birth to Joseph's child with nothing but a wet sheet to protect her from the eyes of the world. The painter gave up his secluded position behind his easel for once in his life and came over to assist the mother of his child. I became a flurried midwife kneeling between them, but when it came time to cut the cord (with a donated fisherman's blade) I was as good as any surgeon at the task.

Joseph wrapped his son in dirty linen and cried real human tears (the kind that tasted of salt rather than stream). Then he embraced us one by one, even the men who had stopped scaling their fish to watch.

I understood for the first time what my friend's blossoming belly had been hiding. I realised that Violette and Joseph were better friends than I could ever have imagined.

I assumed they would now be ready to exclude me, but again I was wrong for our threesome was to continue despite the addition of someone new. Violette told me she and Joseph had secretly married in a civil ceremony a month before, though mutual poverty required them to live apart. After three weeks of nursing her baby, my friend returned to the almshospital (with the infant resting in a sling around her neck). She resumed washing linen in the Rhône, feeding her child in public with only the slightest embarrassment. She continued to rely on me for daily counsel, expecting assistance with mothering the infant.

I felt it was my child which had been born, yet I knew it was not my own. I had allowed myself to be drawn into the lives of my friends but I was still the outsider looking in. When the baby cried for hours it never affected me as it affected Violette. When Joseph and Violette argued about something I could smile weakly and walk away, forgetting what the disagreement was about as soon as my back was turned.

Violette was the lover and mother and through her I was both these things too. I had no wish for the intimacy I saw between Violette and Joseph and Violette and her baby. I saw Violette's vulnerability and I was thankful it belonged to someone else.

(I did not shut her out and she did not shut me out for the door was only partly open in the first place.) Nonetheless we were all grieving for something in our different ways. Especially Joseph and Violette. When a baby is born one way of living ends and another begins.

Joseph treated me with the same courtesy as he treated his wife but he never touched my body. The memory of him covering me with green paint stayed with me as a short sensual interlude which suggested things might have turned out otherwise if the world had been arranged differently. When he came to the fork in the road, Joseph chose Violette not myself and I don't doubt he chose wisely.

It was strength (or the desire for strength) that made me stay with them. Violette was living my life for me (as characters in books sometimes live the lives of their authors), but that fragile part of me which the slightest abrupt wind could render asunder had no greater wish than for this to happen. Violette and Joseph shared their happiness with me partly because I had brought them together and partly because I fully supported their union. I dreamed of a day when I would be able-bodied enough to take my life into my own hands, of a time when I could share the bread of my marriage with others in the same way as my friends were sharing the yeast of their love with me.

Joseph would sometimes rub his hands together and say he and his wife were toughening me up for life. He kept reminding me about how well I had cut the umbilical cord ('No shaking then, was there?'), telling me I was more in control than I realised. When

I got upset about things he'd say: 'Save your tears for something worthwhile, Marie-France,' although he said this more frequently to Violette because she was more of a cry-baby than I was.

I became a privileged spectator to little Fusili's growing and changing. I saw him smile his first smile, cut his first tooth and take his first steps. He had no greater admirer than me for I was his godmother and guardian in every sense except the old Catholic one, though I did baptise him in a 'cult of supreme being' ceremony with fire not water, as was the new republican way.

At twelve months (not twelve days) a bonfire was built in the night air at that very spot where Joseph had first met Violette and where their child had been so rapidly and considerately born. A candle was held up to Fusili's face and the usual prayers were said for his long life and future health. The infant's relatives each took a candle and walked into the Rhône, standing there in a circle around him. The baby swam in a circle of flames. Diamonds danced upon his face.

Further prayers (some old, some new) were said and Violette kept nudging me with her elbow and calling me a high priestess, which failed to amuse me at the time. Far from sitting on a throne like her Highness in the tarot pack (with a crescent moon at my feet and a copy of the Torah peeking from my pocket), I was standing up straight with one very sore hip, reading from a secular document so flat to the ear I had to keep singing sections to give them rhythm and a sacred ring.

After the ceremony I carried the baby home in my arms for Violette was already carrying another child in her womb like a heavy saddle held out in front of her. I changed the little boy's clothing and returned him to his mother to feed. While Violette fed him I patted him to sleep, pressing my own body close against the body of his mother and we were as we would have appeared: two separate women clutching at childhood for contentment. We were hugging Fusili as though the proximity of his small needy body amounted to the ending of sorrow within ourselves.

Violette and I: two countries whose borders were intermingling without conflict. (Joined at the womb but not at the sex.)

'We are becoming each other,' I said to Violette, for I could feel her unborn child kicking me through the walls of her abdomen.

'That is how it was meant to be,' Violette replied, so exhausted she was on the point of falling asleep.

I stood up and went to the door. Joseph intercepted me and we looked at one another as if we each knew something about the other which we did not want (or need) to know. We had an inkling of something (an impossible closeness or unbearable truth) we could not retain in our conscious minds.

'This is not how it was meant to be,' I said to him. He nodded uncertainly and I went out into the night, hunching my shoulders and pulling the spirits of Joseph and Violette around me like bats do their unbelievable wings.

It was my mother who pushed me forward this time and I think her concern was sincere.

'I really think you should make amends with your cousin Emmanuel,' she said a short time after Fusili's baptism.

'He lives in Vienna,' I replied.

'Is that the only reason against it?'

'Oh no. I guess not.'

Long ago I had realised I was clinging to the memory of a *betrothal gone wrong* and my attachment was more to the idea of a severed relationship than it was to my cousin himself. He was still my cousin though. We had a shared history that no-one could deny. Once we had enjoyed each other's company without the commerce of attraction and aversion obstructing us.

There is always a point just before love becomes conscious when it is a secret the heart, stricken by happiness, is keeping from the mind. As soon as it starts to pump its knowledge to the brain, the heart has already started the process of being broken.

I wished to return to that innocent state just before love becomes known. I believed it was possible to go back (a belief inspired by egotism and ignorance) and it was with such a hope in mind that I decided to write to Emmanuel via his mother, my aunt, in Paris. Though France was at war with the Hapsburgs, these battles had been taking place well south of Vienna, in the Italian-speaking principalities. I knew my cousin would have been shielded from our revolution, which was a blessing because his sensitive nature could not have borne much exposure to brutality. In Vienna

Emmanuel might still be the cousin I remembered; in Paris he would have had to remake himself, exchanging his violin for a musket.

Though my mother had been advising me to seek happiness in Avignon, even she allowed herself to be carried away on the tide of my enthusiasm. 'I will go to Vienna alone,' I proclaimed. 'Maybe I will even bring Emmanuel home with me!'

I had been waiting for more than three months for a reply when a letter arrived (via his mama in Paris). It was not a normal letter. My cousin had scribbled his words in between the bars of three pages of music so I had to examine this score very closely to understand his meaning. Certain letters had the appearance of notes and certain rests had found themselves at the top or bottom of letters, giving the words the appearance of a hieroglyphic script.

At the bottom of the first page there was a little gap in the music and here my cousin had apologised for writing on the only paper he had in his possession. (I immediately doubted his honesty on this matter, though anything was possible with the world in its war-torn state.)

It was more likely my cousin had chosen to write on the score because even after all these years he found it easier to communicate through music. I deciphered his words, pulling them off the bars like pegs off a washing line, writing them down again in my own hand on a clean sheet of paper as I wished they'd arrived: in direct, unequivocal speech whose meaning could not be confused.

But what was he saying? I inspected his words (my words now) closely. Emmanuel said he was glad to hear news of my family and to learn I was in good health. He said he would never be returning to his country of birth for there was nothing in France to bring him home. He was happy in Vienna, living next door to a house Mozart had once resided in, playing music in the Freihaus and Burgtheater every night. Then, as if he had no more to say to me in French, he switched to German, a language I barely knew. Surely Emmanuel would have remembered this? I wrote down the foreign words and sounded them out. Of course I couldn't be sure what they meant, but they didn't sound as though they belonged to the cousin I once knew. I was relieved to see the last few lines penned in Italian (Emmanuel's favourite tongue and one which bears such a close resemblance to Provençale I didn't need to translate it). His words of farewell left an impression of lightheartedness which was absent elsewhere. My cousin had warmed up at the end of his letter. He had saved his best lines for last.

There was no return address but on the other side of the score I found a rough map of Vienna. Emmanuel had marked where he was living with a cross. His apartment was in a street running off the Stephansplatz in the centre of the town, right next to or perhaps even part of one of Mozart's old habitats. Why had my cousin given me a pictorial address? I could not write to a picture. With the letter came a considerable amount of money in *Louis d'ors* but it was not clear whether this had come from Emmanuel or from his mother, who had been generous with her inheritance in the past.

It was a deluded twisting and turning of logic in my mind that made me imagine an invitation to Vienna in this inauspicious greeting. Another person might have interpreted it as a tactful directive to keep away.

But if Emmanuel was running cold I was running hot and nothing was going to stop me seeking out my dreams for all of a sudden I found myself wearing the golden fleece of Giselle's passion and the dyed ram's hair of Violette's sensuality. I wanted to frolic in the sunshine. I wanted to acquaint myself with the world. Within a week I had my trunk packed and my coach trip to the capital of the Hapsburg empire booked and paid for in full.

Why my fears had evaporated I wasn't quite sure but I knew it had something to do with Joseph and Violette and needing to stand on my own two feet. Wherever I went in life I would carry them united within me, as though their child Fusili was forever in my arms repealing my absent motherhood. From the moment of his birth the outward signs of my inner turmoil had begun to subside. My tremoring days were almost over.

I must admit I was attracted to the idea of a journey more than anything else. It was a hazardous thing to consider: a woman travelling on her own across France, navigating the Alps and riding east almost as far as the mind could fathom. But I couldn't help myself. I had been reading a book by Mary Wollstonecraft (a recently translated volume which my aunt had slipped into the package containing Emmanuel's letter) and I was determined to follow in the Englishwoman's footsteps, to step outside my country as she had done, following her heart without regret.

I would be leaving in a month. Then I could put my troubled separation from Joseph and Violette behind me. I had continued to see them with increasing discomfort, though not yet with what you might call open rebellion. Neither of them understood my need for independence. Neither of them believed I would be leaving them for something better.

The night before I left Avignon the streets of our town were full of people celebrating the storming of the Bastille prison in our capital city seven years ago. Rowdy revellers waving tricolours cavorted in the Rue de la République where Joseph and Violette stood with hundreds of others, watching the pageantry unfold.

Fusili was sitting on his father's shoulders, laughing at the coloured rain falling down from the sky. Red and blue clouds bursting overhead made him cry out with delight. I was leaving in the morning and would miss the boy as much as his warm-hearted parents. The fact I doted on the infant seemed itself a good reason to go for he was not my child and could never be so.

Feeling hemmed in by the crowd and unable to enter into the jovial spirit of the evening, I took a short walk uphill towards Castle Rock where I could see merrymakers revelling on barges below. Climbing the steps of the bridge I had a view of young girls on the nearby island, dancing a round, bells jangling from the hems of their gowns as the fiddle and mandoline played.

A guard at the pier gate (it was always kept locked at night to protect watercraft moored there from being stolen) recognised me and opened the railings, allowing me to take a short walk upon the bridge's smooth forearm. The river was deceptively still for some reason, perhaps mistaking fireworks overhead for an approaching storm from the north.

I stood at the end of the bridge looking towards Villeneuve (invisible town except for its coquetry of turrets and pretty spires) where gunpowder blasts from the local arsenal were pockmarking the sky grey and pink and white. Our closest neighbours were marking the day in a similar fashion, though on a smaller scale.

Wild children scampered across the river flats on the opposite bank, clutching torches of fire. The smallest of them (probably far too young to be running around at this time of night) dropped his blazing stick and left it behind while he ran uphill after the others.

Two minutes later a distant bush lit up before my eyes, then another and another. Five bushes burned brilliantly (how could we ever have known they had so much fire in them?) then submitted to the tranquillity of the river upon which they had mounted their beauty.

I stood on the bridge looking across at Villeneuve until my female form (I was bareheaded and my figure was no longer obscured by one of those detestable and now out of fashion blossoming bellies) was noticed by swimmers, some of whom called out to me invitingly. I smiled absent-mindedly, opened my purse and threw into the water a handful of small coins which they fought over like seagulls. Then I turned on my heels and, after thanking the gatekeeper, returned to my friends and the clatter of the crowds in the heart of our town. I tried to be merry like everyone else. I tried to convince myself I felt what I did not, but it was a hopeless task for my mind was already gnawing away at its future like a dog upon a bone. My mind was halfway to Vienna, having hurled itself on board a horse-drawn float.

The next morning I awoke and embraced the day as though it were the full glass of burgundy I'd refused the night before. I could not separate my happiness from my unhappiness. I did not really know upon which harp I was playing. I could hardly tell right from wrong, deception from winning artifice (that which is guided by a candid heart). I knew too much to know anything convincingly. I hoped only in that faraway place the meanings would become clearer and I might hear my own voice above everyone else's.

Part 3

Birth

At the salt mines of Salzburg they throw
a leafless winter bough into one of the
abandoned workings.
Two or three months later they haul it out covered
with a shining deposit of crystals.
The smallest twig, no bigger than a tom-tit's claw,
is studded with a galaxy of scintillating diamonds.
The original branch is no longer recognisable.

The Journey

*L*eaving my own country for Helvetia was the hardest thing. As we drove north past moulting haystacks and through the sunflower fields I kept wanting to stop the coach and make my way back home. I held the hands of the other passengers to keep my fears at bay. We played childish games to pass the hours and at first sight of the Alps I closed my eyes and ingested large quantities of aromatic snuff.

In a Grenoble coaching-house, my nerves in tatters, I rested three days, unable to go on. I played hoops and knucklebones with the innkeeper's half-naked children amongst domestic fowls and dirt, longing for someone to bring a message from Papa insisting I return. A two-year-old boy with silken curls reminded me of my brother Emile at that age, and when I held him close, I felt again a strong desire for a child of my own.

I asked people I met what I should do, and they each told me what they would do if they found themselves in my situation. Those who were profiteering in these troubled times told me to continue my journey and find my cousin. The ones facing hardship told me to make do with what I had back in Avignon. The men were usually for adventure and the women were for prudent behaviour, though there was no general rule. I came to the conclusion their advice had more to do with their own lives and how they had lived them and couldn't really help with my own decision.

The innkeeper's wife suggested a visit to the local fortune-teller. The woman lived in a tent at the edge of the town and I found this place and pushed through a web of veils at the door of her cushioned home. She looked like an ordinary woman, a gypsy with a thoughtful brow and a lithe, sinewy frame. I paid her and she lit a perfumed candle and considered both my palms.

'Will I find my cousin?' I prompted.

'You will find him,' she nodded.

'And?' I asked expectantly.

'He will have three heads.'

'Ugh,' I said, imagining all kinds of monsters waiting for me in Vienna. 'Perhaps I shouldn't go on then.'

'It's your choice. Just a moment.' The woman got up and rummaged inside a wicker basket. 'Here, I will give you this ring in exchange for a silver coin.'

She handed me a ring set with a dark red stone which I immediately put on my middle finger. 'It will protect you in future,' the woman added.

Though sceptical, I wondered if I would need protecting. I went along with the charade and asked how I should deal with the enemy, having recognised him as such. She told me to flatter him and remain chaste. And always be certain to wear the ring. I fought back a condescending smile.

'Hold the stone up to the sun and you will see,' she said, lifting the flaps of her tent to let me out.

When I had walked a considerable way from her calico temple and could be sure no-one was watching I took off the ring and held it up to the sun. The stone lit up and I saw a vision of the male Graces from the underwater almshospital. Them again. Well, it could have been worse.

I put the ring back on my finger, musing on this matter as I walked back through the town. When I held the stone up to the sun later in the day it no longer produced a reflection of the three Graces. As it happened they never appeared for me again. I must have imagined the vision. We live in a magical world but once you start believing in it you're truly done for. But perhaps I had broken my own spell. What if the opposite were true, and once you stop believing in magic you're truly done for?

The next morning I was woken by three of the innkeeper's children jumping on my bed. Two of them ran off to bring me my breakfast, which I ate on a tray leaning back against the feather bolsters with the children commenting on my food while I was consuming it.

'You must stay. You *must* stay with us,' said the five

year old, almost strangling me in her effort to make this point.

'Yes, I would like to stay,' I said, cutting up some bread and jam to give her. I was beginning to relax in Grenoble as I became accustomed to the new town and cooler climate, but this sense of calm itself gave me the confidence to continue my journey. At that moment, surrounded by the children's luminous faces, feeling I would like to stay, I made the decision to go on. I'm contrary like that. Violette used to say I was. There might be a perverse element involved in making up my mind, but I think it's mostly about the battle within and choosing what's least harmful for myself and those closest to me.

I said goodbye to the innkeeper and his wife with their five children draped around them like curtains.

'She told you to go on?' the innkeeper's wife asked me in hushed tones outside the coaching-house.

I shook my head. 'No. She guessed my nature I think, then tried to put me off.'

Crack, crack, crack, went the coach driver with his whip as the heaving horses dragged us up a hill then down the other side.

The driver drove fast through the Alps, tearing like lightning along the postroads which thrilled no end the two children I had on board with me from Geneva on. The carriage was fetid and dark for there were no windows. Through fissures in the walls I could see travellers camping by the roadside, tending their sparking fires.

The rain seeped in through the torn leather roof and we had to tie our clothing up like washing to keep ourselves dry. The Genevan children, Rafael and Sophie, stuck their fingers in the holes to help. I was looking after them all the way to Salzburg in the absence of anyone more suitable, and an elderly Helvetian watchmaker with a benevolent air was assisting me with their care. If we didn't always know where we were, at least we knew what time it was for he had three watches around his neck and a packing case full of jumping clocks.

We travelled with three or four soldiers most of the way for many of them didn't care to march across the Alps. The watchmaker made them take off their swords when they came on board. Side by side in their regimental uniforms they sat, chewing on their nails in hunger or fear. At the posthouses, when we changed horses, the infantry bundled out and new infantry bundled in. Some were probably deserters because they were going in the opposite direction than their regiments. (I felt a fondness for these young men, having done some deserting of my own in the past.) Others were merely pretending to be French. They gave themselves away as soon as they opened their brandy-weeping mouths. Prussian mercenaries, victims of the continental wars. The mopey ones with bandages needed special attention from me. Fortunately I'd brought my marigold compresses along.

The children made a list of the soldiers' names and where they were from, which they wrote down in the dark and recited aloud when we stopped at inns for obligatory meals. I corrected their spelling. A favourite was a clarion player who couldn't stop playing tunes; he was known as Maximus of Swedeland, though his real identity remained a matter of some dispute. Needless to say Rafael and Sophie were delighted by his playing but he drove the rest of us to distraction.

For the most I sat in the tunnel-like darkness, listening to the thud of the horses' hooves, the snore of the soldiers, the ticking of the watchmaker's myriad clocks and the lisping of the two children at their melodious chitchat. It was hard to breathe in the carriage but it was comforting enough, like listening to mass in a crowded chapel, knowing everything for the time being is out of your hands.

We slept in alpine lodgings, the pure air cleaning out our congested lungs.

The chaise, a dilapidated waggon from the start, was slowly wasting away, shedding layers of its rotting skin as we rollicked along the rough-hewn roads. Descending the Alps into the low-lying cantons, a whole board ripped off the side and we had a pleasing view of mountains for the first time. There was no longer snow on the tips. The surrounding hills were green. Fewer soldiers hopped on board, but coaches were full of them heading the other way, towards the action.

Stopping in the town of Bern, the coach driver surveyed the damage to the sides and canopied roof of his vehicle. He swore and coughed up a lot of phlegm.

In spite of the situation we'd have to go on, he told us, because items on board were overdue in Vienna. (Contraband, I suspected.) In this modest town with its clear crystal river, I bought Sophie and Rafael bags of boiled sweets. We sat in the sun beside the Münster and I combed out the little girl's hair. It was full of lice. I squeezed the eggs between my fingers and pulled them down the glistening strands. She was so patient, the girl. Rafael wouldn't let me touch his tousled hair, though he was constantly scratching his scalp. 'Tomorrow I'll let you. Tomorrow,' he said, leaping off the bench we were sitting on and grazing his knee. Tomorrow he would be just as reluctant.

Pondering the simple lines and spiritual beauty of the Gothic cathedral, I wondered if I should confess to the children I'd once been a nun. It would change their opinion of me, so I decided against it. I showed them Emmanuel's portrait and they both said politely they thought he looked nice. They showed me a portrait of their godmother, a matronly woman in a frilly white cap who was apparently expecting them in Salzburg in a week or two.

Travelling from Bern to Zürich we lost five more boards from the side of the carriage. We began to feel vulnerable with the sun and wind flaying our skin. I was worried the children would be thrown out if we hit a boulder or dropped down a pothole, so I strapped them both to the seat. At my request the watchmaker took out some tiny nails and a hammering tool from his jeweller's case and started securing the planks that remained. We were making good progress but in

Zürich we lost the watchmaker himself. He alighted at the coaching-house in the normal way, for he'd reached his final stop.

Now there were only the children and myself inside for no-one wanted to board what remained of the fly-away chaise. As we'd already paid for this coach driver (he of the regular coughing fit) we had to continue with him all the way. The watchmaker very kindly left me some absurdly small nails and a hammering implement so I continued to work at the walls of the chaise, but it seemed a futile task and I soon gave up. The children took over for a while. Then *they* gave up and I started again. It went on like that for quite a while, us stopping and starting. (Thinking we could help, then realising we couldn't.)

Nearing Salzburg we struck the wheel of a broken-down carriage and our leather canopy (which had been flapping like a sail overhead for several hours) tore off completely. A gust of wind blew it high away in the sky like a magic carpet. The children looked up with gaping mouths watching it disappear over the top of a hill. Now we were riding along in an open-air cart, which we didn't mind too much because the weather was fine and we could watch the horses and the driver with his flailing whips leaning forward on his seat up in front. The scenery was treed and lush. The villages were all pointed and grey, not orange and spread out like those in Provence. Soldiers in these parts were few and far between.

The base of the chaise was wearing away. The wheels were groaning in disbelief. We could see the road appearing between our legs. Dust was rising through the gaps in the lumber work.

'I hope our luggage doesn't fall off the back of the trap,' said Sophie.

I hope we don't choke to death, I thought. Retaining my composure for the children's sake, I told them the tale of *The Magic Flute*, informing them we would soon arrive in the birthplace of the greatest composer ever born. The latter information didn't impress them overly but they loved the story, especially the dragon and Papageno's foolish ways. We made it to Salzburg with many a hitch along the road. The chaise was certainly losing its britches and we ended up sitting on a few planks of wood over the back wheels for there was nothing else to sit upon. I parted from the children with much affection and firm promises to write and keep well.

Returning to the coaching-house after a night spent in an inn where I cried myself to sleep, I found our driver securing the remaining luggage to the pair of packhorses he'd hired for the final leg of the journey. The weather was closing in. It looked like rain ahead. I chose to sit up front next to Monsieur of the Racking Cough for it was no longer safe in the carriage behind and I'd rather sit next to someone than travel alone.

I rested under a blanket most of the way and when the coach driver pawed at my leg I dug an elbow into his ribs. He wasn't so bad, that driver, despite the occasional lewd suggestion. He was an excellent conversationalist and he had lots of spare covers as well, which was fortunate because when we left

Salzburg it started to rain and never let up. He had some children back in Geneva so I got him talking about them and the discussion softened him. I always think if men have children in their care they can't be too reprehensible. Even though I didn't have any children myself I wanted some. I was missing Sophie and Rafael for we'd shared our cosy quarters for more than five weeks. If the nuns had had children that might have made them easier to get along with. *Nous aussi nous serons mères ...*

I wondered where my fellow Carmelites were now, and whether they were still in Genoa. Perhaps another of our order had broken her vows. (That would make me feel better.) Though unlikely, it was possible they had resettled in Vienna. It might be my fate to return to their fold some time in the future. I considered this possibility for a few minutes then dismissed it, realising my imagination was straining to find a predestined meaning for my voyage. The most obvious meaning (my desire to see Emmanuel again) was too fraught with anxiety to accord it the seriousness it was due.

When I was a novice in the convent I had lots of mothers and I could stay a child forever. I had to give up all thoughts of having a child but that didn't seem such a sacrifice then. I could only think of what had happened to Giselle. If the sisters had wanted to have children, they wouldn't have become nuns in the first place. Claude once told me she would rather be torn apart by lions than let a child take dominion of her body. Most of us, though, were just too young to know what we wanted. Some were pressured into joining, then years later, when the democratic and revolutionary governments encouraged us to leave, were too set in their ways to do so. They'd grown accustomed to each other and convent life.

Loving God every day, or striving to. Praying with abandon, lying flat on the floor, heart thumping against the bare tiles. Submitting to Christ who was *always* worthy of our love. The thought of submitting to a fallible man was beneath our dignity. Seeing so little of men, we regarded them with as much criticism as naivety.

You can't just walk away from those habits and not split into two. You can't not look back. I never regretted leaving the Carmelites. Neither did I regret the early years spent in their midst. They formed my character, for better or worse. They made me solitary, stoical and incorruptible, schooled in the thinking of Joan of Arc. I regretted staying with them so long, wanting to leave but not trusting my own instincts.

I still felt myself a Carmelite even after three years separation. I was connected by my faith and all the memories we shared. I could picture each of the sisters' faces. I could hear their madrigal voices.

I knew that Sister Marguerite would have taken the model city of Avignon with her when they banished her from our land. She may have left her belongings behind but she would have taken the little city. I imagined her stepping on board a barge, carrying the cumbersome building with the help of Catherine and Genevieve. Under arrest yet defiant to the end.

If the coach driver became too persistent I'd tell him I was a Carmelite. I'd show him the crucifix hidden in the locket round my neck. I was hoping it wouldn't get to that because nuns were also out of favour in the Hapsburg lands we were driving through, though not to the same extent as in France. The driver claimed to be a Catholic but he might have been just saying that to please me. I didn't know him well enough to tell and I didn't intend knowing him any better either.

In the end the coach driver wore out before I did. He slumped over in his seat, snoring with exhaustion, ten miles out of Vienna. The horses knew the road well and continued to trot towards our destination though neither of us was working the reigns.

With Vienna finally in sight (a speck on the horizon crowned by a tiny smudge of smoke) I stood up in my seat, holding my hat to my head, watching the town grow bigger and bigger by the minute. I was closing in on the object of my desire after so many years, it seemed now, in exile.

If my cousin had by some misfortune moved to another place I could still see where he had lived. I would walk the streets he had walked. I would hear the music he loved. I might sit in the church where he prayed. If worst came to worst, my journey would have a meaning. Besides, some people say the journey is everything, the destination nothing in comparison.

But what was I thinking? I was going to meet Emmanuel because the fortune-teller had predicted it. Bearing down on the fabled city I was feeling so euphoric I could only believe my fairytale was going to come true. What the fairytale might turn out to be I didn't yet know. I just hoped it would be as good as the ones I'd been telling Rafael and Sophie in the taverns each night to get them to sleep. And the mother in the stories was going to be me this time. I promised myself that.

The horses passed through the city gates and began to slow down. When they came to a halt outside the stable door of their customary coaching-house the chaise gave a sigh and collapsed in a heap of metalwork and sticks. The driver and I fell to the ground, unharmed. (The blankets protected us I think.) We found ourselves sitting amidst straw and dung, bent rods and steel springs. The surviving wheels went rolling away in different directions.

The horses looked around at us, unconcerned. The monsieur offered me his arm and we climbed out of the wreck together. His face, recovering from the shock, was full of pride. He'd brought me to Vienna in one piece, though you could hardly say the same about his hapless vehicle.

8

The Musical City

September 1796

I first saw Vienna through a veil of softly falling rain. The city wore a veil this time, not me, and I never saw her in the daylight without it on. In Vienna the rain had been falling quietly, almost imperceptibly, for several days, for several weeks, for several years as it turned out.

Light rain always fell in Vienna. Never too much or too little. There was always enough water to go around. The Danube never flooded, though little streams ran along the edges of most of the streets because of the incessant trickling down the walls of the buildings. In some of the broader avenues people were walking on duckboards raised over rain-soaked cobblestones. Here where there were no drains the streets were awash (or maybe the drains were blocked by clumps of autumn leaves).

I never saw inhabitants tipping ablution water out of their windows. They were too proud of their sparkling freshwater streets. The Viennese loved their drains and worked relentlessly on their increased efficiency. The sewers were hidden underground and the city emptied itself out each month when every man, woman and child (except for the Emperor and his family of course) took to the streets and swept all the stagnant water away.

I left my trunk with the keeper of the coaching-house and (on a pair of legs that had almost forgotten how to walk) made my way tentatively through the maze of streets, holding Emmanuel's map close to my face. With the rain smudging the ink on the parchment, the further I walked the less chance I had of knowing where I was going. Fortunately I had memorised the street name. I kept asking people where I could find the Domgasse and they kept pointing me in the vague direction of where they thought I should be going.

There were ordinary people with baskets and waggons and children flocking around them, and there were others who were standing very still as though time had frozen them into plaster-cast poses from which they could not escape. Here was a statuelike sentry leaning against a gate and there a wooden woman bending over a cartful of vegetables as though she were stuck there by some inexplicable misfortune. I'd never seen so many statues in my life!

When I cast my eye on these unmoving beings some of them jerked awake and burst into song, surprising me with arias I knew from the opera scores Emmanuel had been sending us over the years. The sentry sang Leporello's indictment of his master from *Don Giovanni* — '"*Madamina! Il catalogo è questo delle belle che amò il padron mio.*"' — and the wooden woman did a fine rendition of Zerlina's plaintive aria from the same opera — '*Batti, batti, o bel Masetto ...*'

When I stopped looking directly at them, the figures stopped singing as suddenly as they'd started, even in midsong. I passed a witchlike woman selling birds in cages and wooden flutes and when I looked at her she began to sing the 'Queen of the Night' aria in German. (Everyone else was singing in Italian.) Her voice was so powerful I continued to stare at her and listen, so that when she finished her exhausting descant and there was no Tamino to take over, she was forced to draw in a deep breath and begin again. Enthralled I couldn't turn away. I wanted her to sing forever. After she'd sung the aria twice, she frowned, scratched her head and told me in Italian she needed a rest. She was singing in the Wiedenhaus that night and she couldn't afford to lose her voice.

I looked away, embarrassed to have made her perform an encore when she was obviously unwilling. I wanted to ask her (as she was working in the Wiedenhaus) whether she knew my cousin, but I wasn't sure whether this would be appropriate — it might be like breaking one of the formalities that exist between a stage performer and her audience.

How odd that in this German-speaking city Italian was the predominant language, as though the divisions between countries had long since lost their relevance. I came upon a soft-faced boyish woman standing perfectly still in the doorway of a storybook cottage. She looked just like the character Cherubino I'd seen in a production of *Figaro* in Avignon the previous year, so I walked up to her and nodded, expecting her to break into a blissful bel canto. But there was to be no musical sustenance from her.

'What are you staring at?' she replied in a low voice. 'Haven't you seen a woman in a pair of man's trousers before?'

This time I turned on my heels and fled. I could hear the woman's mocking laughter at my flight. Worse still I ran headfirst into a soldier who was absent-mindedly polishing his ceremonial sword. In the collision he stabbed himself with his own blade then sang the dying aria from an *opéra buffa* while I crouched over him, praying he be spared such a dismal end. On another level I was unperturbed by his fate, enjoying the richness of his swansong which seemed to be rallying in spite of his wilting pose.

When he did take his final gasp, I knelt down and touched his cheek. It was warm. I touched his blood. It looked and smelt like the juice of some berried fruit. You could see furry seeds swimming in pools of vermilion. He was a very good actor I decided. He was handsome too, so I kissed him on the cheek and he came back to life.

In this new city which had taken me into its arms as

blithely as a Mozart overture I had no fear because I had an instinctive feeling I would come to no harm. I didn't feel invincible. I felt humble and as fragile as ever, but there was a hopefulness in the winning music I heard around me and the look of pleasure on the faces of the singers as they sang. In love with the sound of their own voices they were not in love with themselves. (We cannot help comparing ourselves to others and among this talented throng I felt my own voice to be an ugly quacking thing.)

The stout Viennese moved about at their daily tasks but behind their toil one could find an inner circle of sopranos, tenors, baritones and contraltos guarding and marking the hours as though their individual offerings had replaced the chiming church bells of the past. People greeted each other with the word presto or, more commonly, allegretto. It was a city whose squares were stanzas, whose lampposts were staves, whose cul-de-sacs were elusively trembling treble clefs. The singers were carrying the city's lifeblood in their songs. We sightseers were holding our breath on their dazzling duets and crooning cavatinas. The clouds were composed of ribbons of voices. Released from the lungs of the living they could only float upwards or expire.

The opera houses spilled out their performers onto the cobblestones by day and lured them back at night. Some of the streets were empty of singers. They were like pauses between note-filled bars. Yet wherever I stopped I could hear harmonious tuttis in the distance.

Did they ever stop? There was no-one close by who could answer this question except the singers themselves, and I guessed they would not want to tell.

'Do they ever stop?' I asked a gentlewoman passing in a carriage. She would surely speak Italian.

She bent her head forward through the open window as the carriage slowed. 'Only when the rain does,' she said, or rather sang in recitative, for she herself was one of the nightingale-throated gang. Seated next to her was the very same Cherubino look-alike I had encountered earlier. Why she was now inside this coach I had no idea. When I glanced at her she gave me an impish grin and began the solo I'd earlier wanted to hear.

'"*Non so più cosa son, cosa faccio ...*"'

Cherubino it was, and this time she didn't disappoint.

I couldn't turn the singers on and off at will as I'd first supposed. They were turning *me* on and off at will! Brave old world. I stumbled through the streets with the map tucked inside my waistcoat to keep it dry. When I chanced upon the *drei knaben* from *The Magic Flute* three times in a short space of time (they told me to be a man three times in a row too, which really got on my nerves) I realised I'd been walking in circles. I grabbed the three skinny boys (whose voices hadn't broken and who were certainly not the men they kept prescribing others to be) by the collars of their jackets and made it clear to them I'd give them a coin each if they'd take me directly to the place which had been eluding me.

And the boys were happy to assist.

By the time I found myself in the street marked with a cross, lying in the shadow of a monumental cathedral, I had to remind myself why I'd come here in the first place. Ah yes, I had some old wound to attend to, didn't I? I pulled the map from my clothing and squinted down at the place with a faint mark highlighting it. I compared the map with the distinguished building in front of me.

The house (beside a former residence of Mozart labelled with a wooden plaque) was part of a large building with many apartments on different levels. I had arrived at the place apparently. But at which door should I knock to find my cousin?

Turning my head on one side I looked at the women coming and going around me and it seemed for a moment they all wore multicoloured clothes. The dyes had gone berserk in the rain. It was humid and the thin gowns were sticking to the women's bodies.

It seemed appropriate in a city where voices were loosening themselves from governing throats, that the colours should come loose from the fabrics in which they were enshrined. Crimson dye from my sash had leaked down the side of my plain muslin gown. I noticed a flamelike pattern emerging as swirls of colour spread like a fan across the gathers of my skirt.

I was standing in the middle of the street, hoping that one of the doors would open and my cousin would walk out, when I was approached by a slim and self-possessed looking man who introduced himself as Walter. When I responded he recognised my accent and began chatting to me in my native Provençale.

I assumed he was Viennese but I found out later he'd travelled in many places, was conversant in many tongues and had long ago forgotten the country to which he belonged.

When I mentioned my cousin, pointing to the establishment in front of me, Walter said he himself was a temporary resident in the building. While he did not think he knew Emmanuel, he offered to show me around the apartments. If my cousin was somewhere within we would no doubt find him before long.

I lifted the bedraggled hem of my gown above my boots and we entered the building, side by side.

The first door we knocked at was answered by a short fat man who spoke in a high-pitched voice. He replied in Italian to Walter's greetings and enquiries. It turned out he was a famous castrato called Carollini who performed in the Burgtheater every night. He invited us into his cluttered living room and we all sat down. I began to converse with him in my Latinate Italian. He would surely know my cousin if he was working in the same theatre. Emmanuel? Emmanuel who? Carollini shook his head but this seemed to imply incomprehension rather than denial of acquaintance. What does he play? Carollini just brushed my words away with a dismissive hand as though the mention of a violinist had no place in this haven where voices were celebrated above other musical instruments.

The voluble man didn't seem to want to do anything but talk about himself, as though he'd been waiting all day for us to visit him and had nothing better to do than show us his little trophies, his Venetian horses and the antiquities he'd acquired in the courts of Milan and Trieste on his journey north before settling in Vienna. In each corner of the room stood a classical statue. In one corner a torso of a Greek or an Etruscan woman presided. In the second a statue of a girl with a noble face but no arms. A male centaur held pride of position in the third corner, and a Roman athlete with missing genitalia stood unperturbed and alone in the fourth.

It was a curious experience to meet a castrato. I wondered how he could live any sort of normal life outside the theatre with his voice sounding like it belonged to a little girl (I longed to break the lock in Carollini's throat and let the trapped child fly away). Now he was conversing on nearly every topic you could imagine, even telling us about his lovers! From their names it sounded like they were male lovers, which didn't surprise me for Carollini had almost turned himself into a woman.

The stories Carollini related were full of kisses almost received, embraces desperately attempted and usually not returned. (Many must have found him repulsive.) He proudly told us he had made an enormous number of seduction attempts beneath the windows of handsome gentlemen for whom he sang his heart out. Thanks to the blessings of his voice (and his voice alone, I'd have to presume) his interests were sometimes returned and Carollini's descriptions of the ensuing affaires de coeur became so explicit that at one point Walter leant towards me and covered my ears with his hands. (Castratos were certainly capable of experiencing sensuous pleasures it seemed.)

I interpreted this gesture as protective despite its startling intimacy. Emmanuel, I remembered, sometimes used to cast his hand across my eyes to close them just before he played his violin for me. That action, which I never thought of as seductive, was intended to make me listen to his music more intently. The motion of a hand across the eyes, however, is vastly different from the motion of hands across the ears, for ears are sensitive to touch in an entirely pleasurable way, whereas eyes are always resistant to touch, however favoured the hand that touches them may be. The seemingly modest action of Walter's hands pressing firmly against my ears produced a far from modest response within me, and though I did not let my excitement show upon my face, I hoped that Carollini would continue his salacious tales so that Walter would continue holding my ears.

When Walter finally and regrettably released my ears from his clasp I felt my whole body become as an ear (of corn, of wheat, of hay) waiting to brush against the body of another.

The castrato had moved on to telling stories of the young men who had rejected him, those who had greeted his songs not with applause but with buckets of water. Carollini's vanity was so great he wanted to believe the whole world was in love with him, Walter and myself too no doubt. The ablution water surely only indicated there was a dearth of flowers close at hand.

His vanity was not just limited to his voice. He took an unwarranted satisfaction in his physical appearance and continued to brush his hair and regard himself in the salon mirror while we sat watching him. I found this attention to his appearance disconcerting because he was over forty and not in the least attractive. While Carollini was preening himself Walter told me in hushed tones that the man possessed a remarkable alto. His mature voice was an octave higher than a normal soprano's. It was as clear, pure and penetrating as a choirboy's, yet infinitely stronger and more vibrant.

Now I wanted to hear the castrato sing and, feeling more relaxed (we had been offered pale gold wine in exquisite glasses by an African manservant wearing a turban), I pleaded with him to entertain us. Carollini shook his head and said he had never sung in his chambers yet for he would surely shatter all the crystal in his Louis XV cabinet if he were to do so. He would shatter the wine glasses in our hands and cut our fingers too, he warned. Walter and I put down our glasses straightaway and my new acquaintance offered the alto some money to sing a few scales for my sake, but Carollini just shook his head.

'I'm saving myself for tonight's performance,' he apologised. 'You charming people must stay and keep me company though, for it is only last week I learned of the death of my mother in Rome. It happened some time ago, several years in fact, but I have only recently heard about it. The pain in my heart is great. As a child of ten I had the best voice in the Sistine choir. I was an angelic looking child and my parents couldn't bear the thought of losing me. They conspired to keep me with them always ...'

At this point I tugged on Walter's sleeve and told him I could not stay in the room a minute longer. The castrato's tale was too pathetic. We stood up and departed without saying goodbye for we both knew, given half a chance, Carollini would keep us captive along with his two African boys who were forced to listen to him every day.

We climbed the stairs to the top floor and Walter opened a window, letting in a welcome rush of fresh air. He lit his tobacco pipe whilst I looked across the uneven slope of buildings and drew in some deep breaths. In the distance I could see the river partly obscured by dwellings and the barges moored along its edges. A ship with five masts and misty sails was being guided slowly but persistently into port by a small tugboat and there were gulls flying everywhere like scattered pieces of paper. I knew they would be crying out, those gulls. Even though I couldn't possibly hear the screeching birds from such a distance, their sounds vibrated within me. I put my hand on the cool windowpane and pushed it shut, almost catching Walter's fingers behind the glass.

My friendly escort then took me to a door that led into an apartment where he said some dancers lived. We were invited in by a woman wearing alpine dance costume. An open doorway revealed more dancers and I was surprised to see someone who looked very much like Pedrillo working out at the barre. Looking closely

I realised it actually *was* Pedrillo and he was teaching the girls the same dance routines of the past. So my old teacher had ended up here in Vienna ...

Did I know this man? Walter was surprised. I wasn't mistaking him for my long-lost cousin, was I?

'No, this man isn't my cousin,' I assured him. But just for a moment, as I said this, I did see Pedrillo and Emmanuel merge into one. Were they really different men? Or did each man become like every other in my mind's undiscerning eye? If my own perception (and the contours of history) was colouring what I saw, what chance did I have of seeing a man as he really was? Pedrillo and Emmanuel had both been devoted to music, but that was perhaps the only thing they had in common. Why did I feel all of a sudden that they were attached like spokes to the same emotional wheel whirling within me?

Inspecting the dancers' routine I noticed the jaunty lasses were teaching Pedrillo to waltz. This new dance step was the latest fashion in Vienna according to Walter. Pedrillo wasn't simply the teacher here, he was also accepting instruction from the dancers. I had no wish to make myself known to him again, so I turned to leave and Walter followed.

The next door we came to had a most unusual looking knocker. Two bronze keys were diagonally crossed, one pointing north-west and the other north-east. Walter tapped on the door with this cross-eyed knocker and it was opened by a tiny man who held in his hand a gold painted piccolo sprouting green leaves. This dainty man ushered us into a room where two children were being married before an altar decked with almond buds and blossoms.

'Who are these children?' I asked Walter gravely.

'These are Francesca and Mirando.'

'They are too young to marry.'

'No, they are old souls who have finally caught up with each other after a series of previous lives.'

'What were they to each other then?'

'Twins or lovers separated by death. A parent and a lost child perhaps. Only a bond of immeasurable closeness would be worth resurrecting.'

We watched silently as the children, who were about nine or ten years old, exchanged wedding rings. Then the family drew close around them, showering them with sweetly scented petals. The officiating priest did not seem perturbed that he was marrying mere children. He gave them communion from a hammered gold cup. The cup was not offered to Walter or myself. We seemed to be invisible to everyone except the old man who ushered us in and out.

When we left the room of the reuniting children I told Walter I felt no closer to finding my cousin. I must have sounded dispirited because he took me to his own apartment which was just down the corridor. I did not really want to enter the rooms of a man I had just met, but Walter insisted and I found myself being led inside. My new acquaintance could be very compelling when he wanted to be. To my relief a housemaid greeted us. She made me some chocolate to drink, sat me down on a sofa and removed my leather boots to dry them beside the fire.

The excitement of arriving in Vienna had not yet worn off. I would not succumb to the exhaustion of my long journey till later in the day. Walter's rooms were another sight to be wondered at. They were cluttered with costumes and wigs, antique clavichords, odd clocks and tricorn hats all in a state of either gross dilapidation or fussed-over repair. The room smelt of wood glue, French polish and oil paint, which was comforting because it reminded me of Joseph's rooms back home.

In a large drawing room stage sets from past operas presided. They were being touched up and varnished by Walter as a record for future productions. I picked up a blond periwig hanging at an angle on a stand, sat it on my head and pirouetted across an imaginary stage. Walter made some pedantic comment about it being the wrong wig for that actual set, but nonetheless he admitted it suited me quite well. He said that I should leave the wig on because I would have much more success in Vienna as a blonde. He suggested I try on the particular costume that went with the wig, letting me undress behind an oriental screen erected in one corner. When I emerged he took an objective interest in how the dress looked. He was more concerned with the fit of the costume than whether it complimented my appearance. In the end I don't think he was happy with the result because he told me to choose something else.

When I went back behind the screen to change, Walter went back to sanding one of Mozart's boyhood harpsichords. I trusted him for some reason. He reminded me of my brother Constantine (in physique and nature) and this seemed ample enough reason to believe he was on my side. To deny him, to run from him, would be like running from my own brother. Something I would never do.

When I tried on a very generously made, jonquil-yellow diva gown once worn by the great soprano Mademoiselle Laschi, Walter was greatly amused.

'There'd be room for us both inside that one,' he said with delight.

'But it's a beautiful colour and it feels really nice,' I protested, swishing the many layers of crumpled taffeta around me. I was twelve years old and back in my attic room with Giselle.

'So what?' said Walter throwing up his hands. I told him he was being too fussy and he said that fussiness was a necessary virtue in the costume design business. He asked me to try on another gown. Salvaged from a tragedy it was a macabre looking thing covered with bloodstains. It certainly wasn't appealing but I tried it on anyway and you could have sworn it had been made especially for me. When I was laced up and parading in this gory gown I suddenly burst into tears. It had become too much for me. The long, long journey. Not finding Emmanuel. Trusting a stranger who might turn out to be a big bad wolf.

Maybe Walter was trying to humiliate me and I shouldn't have been enjoying myself with him at all. Walter told me not to fret. He already knew the end of the story because he was clairvoyant (or so he claimed) and he was going to restore my feelings as he was restoring to the keys of the boyhood harpsichord their old sense of touch. (What I would restore to him I wasn't quite sure.)

Walter's mouth seized first upon the bloody wounds on my tragedienne's gown. Then it was my ears (those sensory organs again) and Walter's lips were feeding a river of warmth into them. It was as though my ears had been torn in a dog fight and Walter's tongue was fusing the broken skin together. He worked at the seams of the dress and I desired him too, for he was touching me above my breasts and along the inside of my thighs. Walter was denying me something, while remaining respectful of my maidenly modesty.

At first he used the fabric of the dress to caress me rather than his bare hands. He pushed up my petticoat so that the heavy, almost prickly material of the brocaded gown was rubbing against my legs. He bunched folds of the skirt together and ran them up and down my thighs. He pulled down my petticoat and pulled the skirt up over my face, tightening it across my skin as if it were a mask. (I wasn't frightened because I could breathe under the fabric.)

'I can see how pretty you are, even with a mask on,' Walter said. I could feel his fingers outlining the shape of my cheekbones, my nose, my ears. When he lifted the gown above my face he was smiling.

I closed my eyes. If Walter was going to continue with this lovemaking, I wasn't going to look. It did not occur to me to respond with my own hands and mouth, though I might have done so if I'd thought he wanted me to. There was rhythm to his movements as he tore at the bloodstains on the gown. There were lulls and pauses, when Walter appeared to fall asleep, head resting against my breasts or abdomen.

By the end of the drama I felt we had become lovers even though we had not achieved this in the fullest sense. There was a little happiness and much sadness. Walter had made love to my wounded self while the greater part of me lay there, open-eyed and lonely. In spite of this, the lovemaking had been healing for me, as he had intended it to be. In the coupling of bodies I began the process of detaching myself from my long-held subservience to the memory of my cousin.

When I took off the gory gown and stood before him, uninhibited now, in a plain white petticoat and grey stockings, Walter walked over to an open wardrobe and pulled out something new for me to wear. He held up a costume of the finest crimson silk trimmed with gold braid. I gasped for I'd never seen a dress like it before. Walter said this serene creation could be mine if it fitted me, so I tried it on in great anticipation, but it didn't fit. It was made for a much taller Viennese contralto. Walter could see right down my front and the dress was so long it left a puddle of red silk at my feet.

Walter leant forward and blew on the dress a few times as though he was blowing into an invisible horn. I felt the thin fabric gather together then wrap itself about me tightly like plumes of fire. As Walter, keeper of the four compass winds, continued to blow, the dress lifted and swirled so that hot veils of silk were floating against my cheeks and I had to brush them away in order to see. My body was glowing from head to toe. The dress was crackling and crinkling and shrinking until it had become the right size.

I thanked Walter for the present (remembering all of a sudden the green dress Violette's mother had sewn for me in Avignon). I noticed straightaway there were no seams, buttons or laces of any kind on the beautiful garment (either at the back or front). I had no idea how I was going to take it off, but perhaps laces would just materialise when I needed them.

'The dress isn't very practical, you know. How am I going to get out of it?'

'It's a maze, that dress,' he replied. 'There's a secret way out you'll have to search for.'

I told Walter I was worn out and had no patience for new mysteries. Buttons immediately appeared on the red gown and the fabric lost a little of its rosy hue. I felt sad but I didn't know why. Abruptly (concealing my guilt about what had happened to the dress) I informed Walter I was still keen to meet with my cousin because that's why I'd come all this way in the first place. After a short discussion I agreed to delay the meeting until the following morning.

We found a boarding house for me to stay in, a reputable establishment a street away from the Domgasse, still sheltering under the aegis of the cathedral. Walter said he would make some inquiries, find out where Emmanuel was living and take me there the next day.

As I unpacked my trunk I noticed my hearing had been affected by the events of the day. My ears felt waterlogged as though I'd spent an afternoon swimming in the Rhône. I jumped up and down with my head on one side and a ball of wax fell out of my partially deaf right ear and then another from my left ear as I inclined my head the other way.

I knelt down to pick up the beads of wax from the floor and was surprised to find instead two very real looking pearls lying on the carpet. (Some things about Vienna were just too good to be true.)

At seven o'clock the musical city went to sleep. My newly tuned ears met with a blanket of silence. The opera houses woke up. Their doors were thrown open. The singers disappeared into these hallowed edifices to begin their evening's work.

In the streets people began prattling to each other in plain old Viennese again. I opened the shutters and looked out. The rain had stopped as everyone said it would — just when the singing did. I held out my palm and sure enough not a drop of rain fell on it. The street lamps were being lit. Vienna had raised her veil from her face and was looking out at the night with clear bright eyes. She was watching us, but she did not allow the more curious to look directly at her.

A pigeon flying past dropped something into my palm. When I looked, it was an earring the bird had been carrying in its beak — a small diamond-studded lock hanging from a hook. A tiny key was inserted in the lock, stuck fast by a convergence of melted metal. There was no way the key could fall out of the lock, nor could it be turned. It was fixed there for good. This item of jewellery was probably worth a small fortune. Someone in Vienna would be lamenting its loss, not knowing of my willingness to return the missing earring to its owner in exchange for a string of kind words.

That night I had a variation of my recurrent dream about my mother drowning in a well. I was pushing my mother down with my feet this time. Air was underneath the well, not mud as I had always supposed. I pushed my mother out and she was born in another time. Someone I did not know pulled her body free. And then I could see my mother in a far-off place, clinging to a child that was not me.

That was not my own.

Next morning, when it came time to knock at Emmanuel's door, shyness made me stand back and wait. I told Walter to make the introductions for me while I waited nervously around the nearest corner.

He returned alone with a frown on his face.

'Well?'

'He doesn't want to meet with you, Marie-France.'

'What?'

'He says he doesn't know anyone by your name.'

I wondered whether Walter was telling me the truth. I pushed past him. He tried to stop me, then shrugged his shoulders and merely said, 'See for yourself.'

I knocked at the door. Eventually it was opened by an attractive young woman. When I requested my cousin in broken German she said, '*Ich bin die Frau von Emmanuel*.' His wife? But he didn't have a wife.

I was incredulous. The woman was considering me with concern. A window three storeys above opened and a man appeared holding a carnival mask over his face. I could tell from his shape it was my cousin, though his figure had filled out somewhat since our last meeting and the wig was unfamiliar.

'Emmanuel, it's me Marie-France. Let me in,' I said to him in French.

'*Non vi conosco*,' he replied coldly in Italian. Then he said he didn't know me a second time, in German, his voice lowering and fading away as he pulled the curtains across the window as though it was the end of a theatrical act.

In Vienna we were players in God's opera before anything else. If God in Vienna was a Mozartian God — call him Sarastro, call him an apron-wearing freemason, call him what you will — he held us in his hands respectfully and plucked us for all we were worth. And we responded to his numbered fingering before we did the beck and call of each other or the whims by which we beguiled ourselves. At my elbow a trio of village maidens were cooing a mending coloratura. In the musical city ever-loving choristers would step in to buoy you up before you had time to sink.

The curtains above opened and Emmanuel threw an umbrella out of the window. It landed at my feet and in the shock of its fall opened out like the feathers of a black swan.

'You'll need one of these. It never stops,' he explained in Italian. Then the curtains, and the shutters too, closed again.

I picked up the umbrella. It was raining, though I could hardly feel it touching my skin. In this city rain fell inside your skin. Rain and skin were partners as in a trout quintet. I decided it wasn't raining heavily enough to need an umbrella so I folded its feathers closed. I walked back around the corner to where Walter was waiting for me, leaning against the wall and drawing on his tobacco pipe. When I saw him still waiting there, his true-to-his-word reliability became the most wonderful thing in the world and just at that moment he was worth fifty falsely gesturing Emmanuels.

When Walter saw my look of defeat I had an immediate opportunity to use my umbrella, fending off consolatory kisses and embraces.

'Didn't I warn you?' he said as we walked back to the boarding house.

I nodded.

'If you won't heed advice ...' Now he was really rubbing it in.

Noticing my expression he changed his tune.

'He may come around to seeing you yet.'

'Well, I won't come around to seeing him,' I replied, clutching my umbrella and thinking that this gift, if you could call it such (it was certainly in good working order), was some sign of recognition from Emmanuel.

'That's a parasol not an umbrella, you know,' Walter informed me.

I considered the satiny surface of the dark shade and the smooth wooden handle. Maybe he was right.

'Does the sun ever come out in Vienna?'

'Lots of sun showers,' he promised.

Emmanuel must have viewed me primarily as a lover from the past (a person to avoid and ignore), and not as a blood relative first and foremost as I did him. The sun umbrella was the only sign of acknowledgment that we belonged to the same clan.

I knew only two people in Vienna, one who didn't want to know me and the other who had tried to make love to me while I was wearing a gory gown. Loneliness overwhelmed me. It was easier to walk the streets where even the shopkeepers bargained in falsetto than stay in the quiet of my room where my soul was struggling to convert its coffers of weakness into strength.

I walked beyond the old city walls and wandered through low-lying vineyards, making my way towards the Vienna woods which rose up the slope of a nearby mountain. I continued walking uphill. When I had climbed as high as the summit my body was drenched in sweat. I leaned against a tree and found myself looking down on the world. A huge piece of it anyway. To the south stretched the sweeping plains of Hungary. To the north the Slavic steppes unfolded like a kingsize tablecloth. Directly below, the Danube coursed its way in and out of its hiding place among the fronds of rooftops and trees. Vienna looked small and harmless. It was raining down there and up on the mountaintop too. A light wind swept pine needles through my hair. The sun was slipping down below the windowledge of day.

I told myself I would not be defeated by the chain of events that had attended my arrival. I would not be silenced by the face-slapping of fate or restricted by the patterns of my past. I would fight against my tendency to withdraw, resist my desire to return home as soon as I could. I would make this singing city my home and train my voice to rival all the rest.

Starting to shiver (due to dampness rather than cold), I began my descent as the lights of Vienna went on one by one in the valley below. At night it was a city without spires or belfries. Inside the floodlit opera houses Carollini and Cherubino would be practising their scales. Emmanuel would be tuning his violin. Walter would be arriving at the theatre and handing his hat to a servant at the cloakroom door.

Before God made the singing city it already existed in your own heart. It was the birthplace of consuming love. The hearth that shook out its red and golden locks in the dark and gave vent to its own desire.

9

Fire and ice and a multitude of disguises in Vienna

*W*alter introduced me to Viennese society and we became partners at the gaming table, in the home of the very hospitable Count Franz Walsegg. Walter seemed to know exactly what to do in such élite company, whereas my ignorance of the local language and aristocratic custom made me feel diffident and I refused to play alongside him at first.

While he sat at the tables rolling the dice and shuffling the cards with consummate ease, I stood behind the richly dressed players, noticing how their hair colour reflected the drinks on the trays the servants were holding. This one had brandy curls, that one a champagne pompadour. I sometimes peeped at their cards and whispered my findings back to Walter. Each time I assisted him he gave me a heart from his favourite pack, until I had every heart in my possession.

The card players didn't notice Walter was dealing with a heartless pack because he had filled it out with low-numbered clubs. This unbalanced pack seemed to adversely affect the behaviour of the players. They became increasingly aggressive (even the gentlewomen), sometimes hitting and punching each other when they lost. Walter and I were both horrified. 'It's the clubs that are making them do that!' I said to my friend. He agreed, telling me to give the hearts back immediately, which I reluctantly did.

One gentlewoman continued to respond violently when she received a hand with three or four clubs in it, so Walter produced a tamer German pack from last century and we played with acorns (for clubs), and bells (for spades) and leaves (for diamonds) and hearts (as usual). The gentlewoman arrived the subsequent evening with a gown made entirely from twigs. She looked like a giant butterfly cocoon and she twittered all night in the mellowest mood.

There was barely an evening when Walter did not escort me to an opera, to a party or to the home of Count Franz Walsegg. He never thought to stay in after eight and read, or play music. In his company I became more daring, for the eccentricities of Walter's behaviour didn't make him unacceptable to others. Every afternoon a postman would knock at the door, loaded up with parcels containing fancy dresses and props for the night ahead. When a lion cub appeared in a cage with the afternoon mail, it came as no surprise, though Walter hadn't forewarned me of the animal's imminent arrival. I staggered up the stairs with the cage.

'Life in Vienna is one long carnival,' Walter said, taking the heavy cage from me. There was sadness around his eyes though, suggesting a less convivial past. I did not like to ask him questions of a personal kind because I was worried he would tell me something I didn't want to hear. Perhaps there was a troublesome history he was currently escaping.

'I'm picking up some of your powers,' I said to Walter who had been dressing up as Strength, a female character in the tarot pack, for the evening ahead. At Count Walsegg's we had been playing *tarocchi* (a card game using tarot cards) and I had been winning every night.

'I'm returning your powers to you, their rightful owner,' he replied, taking the lion cub out of a cage and attaching a velvet lead to the collar around its neck.

After I'd been living in the new city for two months I received a card from Emmanuel. He said he would meet me beside the left aisle confessional in the Stephansdom the following day. When I arrived at the confessional box five minutes after the appointed time I couldn't see my cousin anywhere. Then I heard his voice from inside the tall wooden box. I tried to enter the confessional but my cousin wouldn't release the curtain. He asked me why I'd come to Vienna.

I told him I'd come all this way to see him but I wasn't having much luck. He told me the nun selling indulgences in the porch had a special message for me. I walked over and introduced myself but she said she was selling indulgences and that was all. When I returned to the confessional my cousin had fled. I went home to my lodging house feeling very confused.

Most days I assisted Walter with his musical restorations for he paid me amply to do so. One day when he wasn't looking I put the gory gown in the fire and watched it slowly reduce to cinders, making the noise of ten firecrackers as it did so. (The metal buttons must have been responsible for this.)

Walter guessed what I'd done. He seemed to be able to read my mind, or perhaps it was my face for my expression always bears the stamp of truthfulness. (I only ever live from one moment to the next.)

'The past is worth preserving in all its guises,' he admonished me.

'Horrible things aren't worth keeping, not even for posterity's sake,' I responded.

'That gown wasn't yours to burn.'

I conceded him this point but refused to admit any fault in my action so our discussion came to an end.

Walter was a puzzling person, alternatively oblique, then soul-searching, then jocular. Once, when we went to the opera, he made me dress as him and he dressed as me with my ruffles and lace. When we sat in the box with our eyeglasses raised, he asked me if I desired him more or less in his fancy female dress. I discovered

I desired him more, but this was only because women's clothing is more voluptuous than men's.

'I desire you more now you're dressed like me,' I replied frankly.

'I had thought you desired *yourself* too much,' he responded. I was mystified by this comment. Was it a query or a statement? I wasn't sure so I quickly put it out of my mind. As a woman Walter wasn't that appealing. As a man dressed up as a woman he was immensely attractive because I knew he was a man underneath those flounces and frills, and the deception was part of the allure.

Dressed like a gentleman I had to behave like one in public. Walter let me smoke his tobacco pipe and I gave him most of my cognac to drink. During the second act I undid the ribbons on Walter's dress and before the next interval I occupied myself tying them back up again. I told Walter he made a sensational blonde, which he did because he had very pale Nordic skin. In the darkness of the third act we exchanged wigs and when the lights went on we swapped them back.

I received a second card from Emmanuel a month after the first. He arranged to meet me on the steps of the town hall. I arrived five minutes late but there were no men in the vicinity, only women buying and selling. One of them, dressed like a mummer, had a dark veil over her face. She moved close to me and softly said my name, or a close approximation of it: 'Marie de la France.' It was my cousin and I wondered why he had pronounced my name incorrectly.

'Why are you still in love with me after all these years?' he asked. Spoken by an apparent woman the question wasn't so offensive.

'You are my cousin,' I replied, but I knew that wasn't the real reason. It is because I hold on to things. I hurt myself and hold on to things when I should really let them go.

'Buy some chestnuts for me please,' Emmanuel said, giving me some money. I went and bought a bag of chestnuts and when I came back my cousin had disappeared again.

Walter didn't seem to care whether I met up with my cousin or not. He had shown no particular interest in seducing me after that first day. He was going to look after me though and was genuinely concerned about the coldness of my hands, which no summer sun or fleecy gloves could warm.

'I have a statue's hands,' I sighed, for I was accustomed to them.

'We'll try something different,' Walter said and packed both my hands inside a cushion of crushed alpine ice. This solution worked, for when I withdrew my hands they were warm, but they only stayed warm for the length of time they'd been in the ice, then they returned to being cold.

'Our Viennese winter will work wonders for you,' he predicted and I hoped he was right.

Walter had the opposite problem. Some evenings when the singing and the rain stopped, his body began to burn and he'd have to take off most of his clothes and fan himself down. Instead of breathing out smoke when he puffed on his pipe he breathed out fire. He's a dragon, I thought, or a wizard perhaps. I'd pour a cold bath for him and he'd get in with his underclothes on for modesty's sake and sweat it out, moaning and carrying on as though he was roasting on an underworld spit. After fifteen minutes, when I dipped in my hand, the water would be boiling.

Walter would jump out of the bath and run dripping down the corridor to find his clothes, his body temperature back to normal. The cold bath had done the trick. I would lock the door, undress and get into the hot oily bath smelling of Walter and the emulsions of his body. I breathed in his musky vapours and almost passed out in the heat.

Later, when I went back to my boarding house and got into my own bed, Walter's oils came out of the pores of my skin and scented my sheets. In his absence I grew drunk on what little knowledge of his body I took pride in knowing.

My senses were returning. (Wisdom had finally allowed them in the front door.) I could smell my own skin and the changing cycles of the day. Morning, noon and night, each had its own moisture and fragrance. The freshness of rain and the perfume of grapes wafting down from the hillsides filled me with purpose.

Expectantly, I basked in a happiness before it was due.

I received a third note from Emmanuel a month after the second. He told me he would meet me on the summit of Kahlenburg the following day. I climbed the hill and arrived at the meeting place five minutes late. I walked around but there was nobody to be seen, only a few goats feeding on wet grass. Then I heard a voice shouting from the top of a sightseeing tower. It was my cousin but I couldn't understand a word he was saying. He was shouting and I started yelling back. This went on for ten minutes or so.

I went to the door of the tower, intending to climb to the top, but I found it locked. My cousin must have taken the key inside with him. I heard footsteps on the stairs and the lock turning. The door opened and I was confronted by a farmer who looked at me in some alarm. He came out of the building and hobbled off down the hill.

After a minute I realised the farmer must have been my cousin in disguise so I chased after him, calling out, 'Emmanuel, Emmanuel!' The farmer stopped and turned around. He shook his head, pointed to the tower and said that the Frenchman was back there. He was right because just at that moment the door to the tower opened again and my cousin, dressed as himself, emerged then disappeared into the pine trees sloping down the other side of the hill.

I was too frustrated to chase after him. Perhaps I should have pursued him. Who knows? Perhaps he had something important to say to me that day on the hill. (If only my hearing were better!) But I was distracted by a rabbit running by and it made just as much sense to follow its tracks instead.

I did see my cousin in the future though. I saw him playing his violin in the orchestra pits of Vienna and I saw him walking down the street, but he didn't look like the Emmanuel I was attached to, the one I had known in Avignon. If he had continued with his disguises I might have stayed in love with him. But the man I kept seeing didn't look very much like the cousin I remembered. My feelings were for another man who was never going to be found.

One night Walter took me backstage at the Burgtheater to meet the singers who had been performing *Così Fan Tutte*. I was surprised to find them lying on the floor with their laces undone and their eyes closed tight. You could tell they were opera singers because they were breathing in and out in a formidable fashion, their chests rising and falling like bellows.

'What's happening?' I whispered.

'First they drink, then they rest and some fall asleep. Then they wake and eat,' an attendant informed me.

Fiordiligi (or rather the singer who had played that part) picked herself up and put on a wrap. 'You were magnificent,' I said, because that's what you should say to the lead soprano after a performance.

'Marie-France!' the woman said with amazement.

'Claude!'

We embraced.

'Is Angelica in Vienna too?' I asked.

'Yes, most of the academy are here, even Pedrillo.'

'I know that,' I said, unenthused. 'You were singing with a middle C,' I said curiously.

She smiled a secretive smile. Then she took me by the arm and led me to her dressing-table where she sat down and began to brush out her hair. 'It was there all along, jangling around inside my voicebox. It had become separated from the other notes. I coughed it up shortly after we arrived here.'

'What did it look like?'

'Like a very small black beetle. It went buzzing around in perfect tune. Zzzmmm ... How glad I was to hear that note again, even if it was coming from outside and not from within. The dancers went chasing it for me. Angelica caught my middle C in her hands just before it flew out the window, and I swallowed it like a potion with a glass of milk. Luckily the note settled back in the right place and here you see me, Fiordiligi.'

'Unbelievable, Claude,' I said, quite sincerely. Then I asked for news of my little friend.

'Angelica has confided in me a passion for ...'

'Bullfighting,' I butted in. Claude nodded and went on to say that Angelica had been rehearsing a nonsinging part in *Don Giovanni* in which she would indeed get to dress as a matador and wave a red rag at a chimerical bull.

'It's not the same as the real thing though,' I objected.

'My child, you wouldn't want it to be.' Claude was sounding just like a mother superior again. Regarding me closely for the first time, she said I was looking happy and must be faring well in this new city. She admired the red gown I was wearing.

'You have found yourself ...' She gestured vaguely in the direction of Walter who was having a conversation with the recently risen Dorabella.

'Not a musician, a magician,' I explained, feeling very pleased with myself.

Claude didn't bat an eyelid. 'In that case we must celebrate with champagne,' she said, tapping a closed fan against her hand and calling for service.

'Your past coming back to haunt you?' queried Walter as we left the opera house in the early hours of the morning.

'I guess Violette and Joseph will be turning up next.'

'I would make myself invisible in that case,' said Walter.

'Don't worry. They belong in Avignon, not here.'

In my boarding house the next day, I picked up two more pearls (which had fallen out of my ears) from the rug at my feet and added them to my store of twenty-four. With the pearls and my card-table winnings I was doing quite nicely for myself.

'Who are these men, indecently dressed in swirls of smoke?' inquired Walter. He was looking into the red stone of the ring the gypsy fortune-teller had given me in Grenoble. I pulled my hand from his clasp. 'They are the male Graces of Avignon,' I answered, staring into the stone eagerly but seeing nothing myself. 'I worked with them in the underwater almshospital.'

'The middle one looks a little like me,' claimed Walter.

'None of them looked anything like you,' I snapped, for he had spoken in a self-satisfied way. It's true one of them *had* looked like Walter from memory, but this was probably mere coincidence. Besides, Walter was much taller than the male Graces, and he didn't have olive skin.

My friend took my hand back forcibly and looked into the stone again. 'The one on the right is about to come into your life,' he said.

'No, he isn't,' I said, snatching away my hand and pulling on a glove. It didn't seem fair that Walter could see the male Graces when I couldn't, and I certainly wasn't going to let him think he could fathom my future. Yet he continued to fascinate me because he had access to layers of reality existing behind the most obvious.

'In nine years time Vienna will be razed by an invading army,' Walter told me.

'Turks?' I inquired, hardly caring who it would be.

'Your countrymen,' he replied, almost accusingly.

If my friend had a fault, it was to be always noticing and pointing out the worst of things.

'Why do prophets always foretell bad news?' I complained.

'In general, news is bad.'

'I knew you were going to say that,' I replied.

'Then why did you ask?'

Winter came (a winter colder than I'd ever known in the south of France), the Danube froze and Walter taught me how to skate on ice, which was something I'd always wanted to do. I hated the blistering cold and I've always learnt things slowly, but by the beginning of Lent in my muff and mittens, with a hood on my head, I could keep up with him if I hitched my skirts high and didn't look down. I was the first on the smoking ice before the church bells rang out and the last to hop off it each night, and I made for myself a special skating hat with a lantern inside so I could stay on the ice when darkness set in. Walter could always see me with my miner's light on and a company of dizzy moths delighted in finding me too.

I belonged to the ice, and the ice belonged to me.

March approached and crystals hanging from the twigs of branches broke like sparrows' eggs against the ground. Boats frozen against the snow-bound sides of riverbanks began to rock themselves awake. Fewer skaters turned out to brave the slippery straights. Even the ice was looking more like glass than the real thing. You could look right through and see the water moving beneath. I saw a woman swimming close to the surface, her long hair wrapped around her, a twisting silver bridal veil.

'It is a woman,' I exclaimed.

Walter shook his head. 'It is a corpse,' he said sadly.

That may be true, I thought. For after death the hair grows and grows and loses neither its lustre nor the thickness of its twine.

'Death is never more than an apparition,' Walter added soothingly.

We left the ice to melt and walked along the riverbanks. In the trees robbers were hanging upside down by their ankles. (This was their only punishment.)

'At dusk the guards will untie them and bring them safely down,' Walter told me.

The robbers floated in the breeze in ballooning gauze gowns and white pantaloons, fumbling with each other, reaching out their hands to touch us and giggling as we strolled past.

'We look silly to them,' I said, starting to giggle myself.

'Yes, but you should ignore them, Marie-France.'

'Why?'

'Because if you play along with it, they'll only want to steal again.'

Walter and I had moved beyond desire. My body and its needs seemed irrelevant and foolish. I'd lost track of chronological time. The seasons were reversed and winter was about to be followed by autumn. The naked spire of the Stephansdom blossomed with orange leaves then rose all the way to heaven. It pierced through the banks of cloud. People were climbing up and down at their leisure, though some flew off before they reached the top, eager to test their powdered gold wings. It was a daytrip only, though you could stay longer if you wanted to. Those who returned said it was little different up there from our world down below.

'It is like the rapture of Saint Teresa,' I told Walter. '*La Santa* says it comes like a strong, swift impulse.

You see and feel this cloud, or this powerful eagle, rising and bearing you up with it on its wings.'

'It is something like that,' he conceded.

The heavens were hanging upside down, raining pollen on us. Voices were streaming into the mouths of the opera singers as if they had originated somewhere in the sky. The tenors and contraltos had their mouths permanently open, fertilised, or waiting to be fertilised, from above. In Vienna there are no seams between earth and sky, between man and woman. No horizons any more.

Walter's dreams turning up in mine like we were drinking from the same stream each night. More pearls on the floor. And now the burden of these heavy, imported wings. What an effort to lift oneself up, and harder still to come down again when you wanted. When it came time for me to try on a pair, I flatly refused.

'When you leave, will the world still be like this?' I asked Walter.

'If you want it to be.'

'I haven't written to my family in weeks.'

'Is that the only thing you're worried about?'

In the park a small girl was being wheeled along in a tiny cart pulled by two German shepherd dogs. The girl was inside a cage of sorts, attached to the cart. A priest walked behind her, lips tightly sealed. I smiled at the girl. Seeing me, she held up two bleeding thumbs.

'You torture children in this place?' I said to Walter judgmentally.

'You're short-sighted. Here she comes again.'

The small girl passed by on her cart a second time, closer to where we were standing. She was outside the cage now, a parrot visible inside. The child was wearing bright red gloves. Behind her walked the priest in conversation with a reverend mother. Behind them strolled a couple of nuns from the local orphanage and half a dozen other children too.

'Her thumbs were bleeding. I saw them.'

'Were you seeing the past or the present?' asked Walter.

I no longer knew, but I hoped it wasn't someone's future I was imagining.

It was the first time I wanted to return to Avignon since arriving in Vienna. I tugged on my leash and found it broken.

'She doesn't have a mother,' I said lamely as the girl and the cart come rolling past me a third time. She was lying on top of the cage now, making faces at the bird.

'She doesn't have a father either,' he said, and I wondered how he could be so sure about this.

Walter was preparing to leave the musical city. He told me his work here was nearly complete. (My ears began to ring.) He had two mistresses and several children waiting for him in Prague. (Cherry stones on the floor instead of pearls.) There was a Polish baroness he owed allegiance to a little north of that fine city.

I found out so much then wanted to know no more. I wrung my hands and despaired. I called him a scoundrel and he made me take it back. I must be fair for he was very generous to me. At his invitation I moved into his apartment and took charge of his opera sets. I sold all my pearls and was able to purchase a singing maid, one of those local delights no cultured Viennese could do without.

In typical Walterian fashion my magician friend departed in a puff of smoke, having made a wish to return to a former time and place. He recited his incantation while standing directly under a spouting fountain in the Rathaus Park. When he vanished, the ground shook and the fountain cracked in a hundred places. The pipes below were damaged and the water stopped flowing immediately.

I walked through the park slowly, as if smothered by a sandstorm. The marble statues on either side of the pathway had toppled from their plinths. A gardener was kneeling before the ruins of the Empress Maria Theresa and when I paused beside him, wrapping my shawl around my head so that only my eyes were visible, he looked up and said: 'Earthquake. Strong enough to flood the Danube.'

'All the statues are broken,' I said in dismay.

'Not the bronzes,' he replied curtly.

When I left the park I found the rest of the city unaffected. Everything was as it had been an hour before.

10

Cherubino's kindness

I did not miss Walter, for the day he disappeared the aforementioned singing maid moved into his apartment. I had acquired Cherubino (the very same character actress who had taken my fancy on the day of my arrival) from a neighbouring countess (a real one, not the trussed-up songstress who had passed me that day in her figurative coach) and this boyish and cheeky maid adjusted to her new mistress and employment with bounce and flair.

She sang for me in her quivering contralto while she dressed and undressed me, and perfumed and pampered my own dark hair. She knew the whole of *Figaro* off by heart and serenaded me in the bath with the entire first act, singing the male parts almost as well as any warbling baritone or entertaining tenor could.

She had an amazing falsetto range and that wasn't the only surprise she had up her sleeve, for Cherubino turned out to be more of a child than I was myself. She frequently clowned around when she should have been pressing my velvet capes or twisting the curls of my brash blonde wig. Returning from the theatre one night I found her asleep in my very own bed.

She was regular with my meals I must admit, but she'd pile the sideboard with more than I could possibly eat. Then she'd sit down and finish what I'd left on my plate. If I upbraided her she'd smile and say, 'Every good girl deserves fruit.' Cherubino wanted to serve me well and she tried very hard, but she made a better singer than she ever could a maid. In the latter capacity she'd always choose to do things the lazy way, though she showed much imagination with the shortcuts she took. When I asked her to shorten the hem of my gown (skirts were still going up in Vienna), instead of using a needle and thread she took half a dozen of my brooches and pinned them inside the fabric to achieve the same effect.

'Now I have no brooches to wear, Cherubina.' I sometimes called her by the feminine and sometimes the masculine form of her name, usually in response to the pitch of her voice (whether it was high or low).

'You never wear those brooches anyway,' she answered back.

When I wanted a drink of water she'd just stick a glass out of the window and stand there going, 'Dum de da, dum de diddle dee dee', tapping her merry foot until the glass was filled with rainwater. Once when she had her arm stuck out of the window in this fashion something other than water landed in the glass.

'Looks like you've scored something else for my efforts today, my lady,' she said, fishing a diamond earring from the glass of water. Astounded, I told her I had the matching pair to that earring and she nodded and said she knew that — she had long ago made herself familiar with the contents of my jewellery box. She quickly located the other earring and offered to put them on me.

'But one of them belongs to you,' I told her. '*You* found it.'

'Yes, but I don't have pierced ears,' she said and lifted the sides of her red wig to show me.

'Alright, just for today then,' I acquiesced, for I prefer to dress without ostentation during the day. Cherubino took the tiny things and very carefully slipped them through the holes in my ears. And then she put up my hair and I glittered and twirled and ran back and forth from my mirror all morning. I think she got sick of me doing this because she took the mirror off the wall and hung it around her neck. Now she was walking around wearing a three-foot long mirror which kept glinting like a suit of armour as it swung against her. I was chasing her up and down the stairs to admire myself and she was doing her chores awkwardly with the heavy mirror on.

She paused for a few moments then put aside her mop and bucket. The mirror was drawing me towards it like a magnet. I embraced the mirror as though it were her, only I was really embracing the reflection of myself.

'Catch hold of yourself and you'll catch hold of me,' Cherubino flirted. I danced backwards a few steps, I danced forward. Cherubino then manoeuvred the mirror around me like a shield, never letting my eyes settle on my beloved diamonds for more than a few seconds. When she finally put the mirror back on the wall she said: 'Why are women so vain?' and I told her that she should know as well as I. Besides, some men were more vain than women. I told Cherubino to go count the mirrors in Carollini's chambers and she raised her eyebrows and said, 'Yes, but what sort of man is he?'

Waking earlier than was my custom one morning, I went down to the kitchen to find some bread to eat but there was none in the pantry to be found. (What a lazy maid I had in my service.) I called for Cherubino but she didn't come, so I threw on a cloak and went for a walk to the baker's shop myself. (The morning streets were quiet, the singers asleep and the sky before rain an almost-forgotten turquoise blue.) I breathed in the sweet smell of yeast in the baker's shop and bought a loaf, still warm from the oven. Returning home and swinging my basket I was thinking how I might go shopping this early every morning, it was such a peaceful time of day, when I passed a barber's shop and was struck by the sight of my maid's brown coat and red wig hanging from a peg near the door.

And there she was, sitting in a black leather chair, a sheet tucked in round her neck, short cropped hair, her face all a lather and froth. Being shaved by the barber himself!

I rushed home, bolted and unbolted the door five times, ran upstairs, laughed then cried then wondered what on earth I was going to do.

'Cherubino, you're not the maiden you said you were.' I decided direct accusation would be best.

'Oh. So it *was* you I saw passing my barber's.' (His voice dropped an octave in reply.)

'You deceived me all these months,' I accused.

Cherubino said nothing.

'You've seen me in my bath,' I said indignantly.

'Yes, every week,' he answered.

'You've touched my person,' I said with disgust.

'Yes, frequently,' he nodded, unashamed.

'You even let me get attached to you!'

At this point he decided to defend himself. He said I had deceived myself and that Cherubino was always a young man to be played by a woman. He reminded me that in the opera Cherubino was an untrustworthy scamp, hiding in his mistress's closet, jumping out of her window and allowing himself to be dressed like a doll from the countess's hanging garden of round-the-world clothes. What my singing maid had done was perfectly in character with the character himself. It was Cherubino I had purchased and Cherubino I received in exchange for my hoard of precious pearls.

'That's a weak excuse if ever I heard one,' I retorted. 'Confusing art and life.'

'There was no other way into your life, Marie-France. I observed you from a distance. I became your maid as a means to an end. You can't close the door on me because you really are attached.'

'I'm attached to a woman,' I insisted.

'You're attached to *me*, regardless of my sex.'

And over this last point I pondered a great deal. What I made of the issue would decide whether I kept Cherubino under my roof or showed him the door as I first intended. He had done something completely unethical which reflected poorly on his character. What point would there be trusting someone untrustworthy? Yet his heart was in the right place. And I would have been bored without him. In the end I told Cherubino that until he went back to being my opera-singing maid I wouldn't be his. Cherubino was happy to oblige and when he got into bed wearing one of my lovely dresses I said to him, 'You're not a man, you're only my maid Cherubina.'

And he said to me, 'When you wake up in the morning you're not going to be scared of yourself or of me, or of the future or the past, or of ...' (The list was lengthy.)

We wallowed in the quicksand of love. Consuming quantities of cakes and Turkish sweets, my waistline started expanding rapidly. Before long I was broad enough to fit into Mademoiselle Laschi's famous golden gown. Thankfully Walter wasn't here to ridicule my wearing it. In my dreams the magician became more and more emaciated, then stopped appearing altogether.

Cherubino and I loved with our hearts and our bodies and we had every good reason to do so. After a time we were more frequently found wandering the Vienna streets than locked away indoors for we wanted to share our happiness around. On a special feast day my maid dressed as a clown and sang his way through the crowds, balancing a plate of honeycombs on the end of a stick. We watched the Viennese with the miracle wings floating down from the sky so slowly, like coins through water.

'Would you like to do that?' he said to me, tipping his plate of honeycombs so they fell into the hands of some attentive waifs.

'Not particularly,' I replied. 'You have to go up first and I might get stuck up there and never be able to come down.'

'Want me to try for you?' sang Cherubino in a faltering descant, flapping his arms foolishly for my benefit.

'No,' I mumbled, chewing on spun sugar, 'you're not Walter and you wouldn't be able to.'

Cherubino looked hurt.

'How do you know I'm not Walter? I could be Walter returned in disguise for all you know. Now you see me, now you don't,' he said and ducked behind a caravan.

I ignored him and kept walking. We almost bumped into each other two market stalls further along for Cherubino had run on ahead then circled back.

'Don't make fun of Walter. It might be bad luck,' I warned.

'I wish you'd never told me how you felt about him. And I wish you'd never told me about Emmanuel. He's still living in Vienna, isn't he?'

'Once I stopped thinking about him, I stopped running into him, so I wouldn't know. Now why did you mention his name? You're not going to believe this, but there he is!'

This time it was I who ducked behind a caravan. Cherubino followed. A dwarf opened the back door and considered us suspiciously. Two grubby toddlers squeezed past him and rolled down the stairs.

'Which one, which one?' Cherubino demanded, peering round the edge of the caravan, refusing to be intimidated by the proprietorial dwarf.

I looked into the crowd and discreetly pointed Emmanuel out.

'Oh, not so bad looking for a Frenchman. He's with a woman who's having a baby!' Cherubino sounded titillated.

'Like someone else you know,' I demurely replied.

'Wait here,' Cherubino told me and disappeared into the crowd. The last I saw of him he was clinging to the tail end of a musical band.

After fifteen minutes he returned puffing, all excited.

'I picked his pocket,' he chirped, pulling a tatty wallet out of his baggy pants.

I looked aghast. Cherubino offered it to me. I refused to take it, so he opened the wallet himself. It was empty except for a note scrawled on a piece of paper which he read out aloud: *Sorry to disappoint you.*

Cherubino couldn't hide his disappointment. He swallowed hard then went on and on about how he'd been swindled. I had to laugh for it served him right. I'd never seen him look so crestfallen but I didn't feel like comforting him.

I liked Cherubino best because he was nothing like Emmanuel — he was never cruel or distant. He rarely withheld his affection and if he did, it was short-lived and not deliberate. It seems ridiculous to love someone most because they are *not* like someone else but this is bound to be the case when you're reacting against a drawn-out and doomed affair. Sometimes it's easier to cling to the safety of dead feelings and another's weaknesses, I decided. A rejection becomes a stronger reminder that one has loved than the remembered pleasure of receiving a treasured violin.

The living Cherubino had plenty of flaws, enough to make Walter seem a perfect saint. He would do naughty things to get my attention. Perhaps that was his worst fault, always getting into scrapes and usually implicating me as well. He was incorrigible but I forgave him because he adored me and intended no harm. Much of the time Cherubino looked up to me, which was very flattering and a change from Walter.

My maid actually preferred to dress as a woman. It wasn't for variety or fancy dress, as it had been for Walter. Feminine clothes suited Cherubino because he had a fleshy figure and refined features. After he'd visited the barber his skin was very smooth. Dressing my maid was the most amusing hour of the day. Slowly I rolled on thick stockings.

'So Herr Lietgeb won't know what hairy legs you have,' I said, keeping a straight face.

Then I put frilly underwear on him, three pairs of frothy lace. 'So Herr Starling won't know about your extras if his hand goes roving,' I explained.

Then I padded his chest with soft bread. 'So you can truly be my bosom companion.'

Then I tightened his stays. 'So Signor Moreno won't know how chubby you are.'

I slipped a petticoat over his head which stretched tight across his shoulders. Cherubino helped me button it up.

'So, so, so. So what am I going to wear today?' he mimicked, lifting the petticoat to admire his shapely legs. This was my favourite part, selecting a gown for my maid. Thanks to Walter's costume collection we had a great choice. Cherubino was the most theatrically dressed servant in Vienna. Wardrobes, three layers deep, with doors at the back and front and at either end. I was inside for half an hour one day, searching for a pink cloak with a fur collar I'd worn once but had never been able to find again.

'You're not still looking for that coat?'

'I know it must be in here somewhere,' came my muffled reply. Eventually I emerged, without the cloak for the hundredth time.

'Why does it mean so much to you?' Cherubino inquired.

'I don't know, it's important for some reason.'

Cherubino climbed into the wardrobe himself and rummaged around in the dark. 'Is *this* the coat you've been looking for?' he asked when he reappeared.

'Yes, that's the one,' but my bright smile faded quickly. The coat was too small for either Cherubino or myself. It would probably have fitted a thirteen-year-old girl.

'I've worn that cloak before,' I said stubbornly.

'A happy memory then?'

'I think it was something sad.'

'You're too old to wear pink, Marie-France.'

Cherubino was quite contented playing my maid, even if he couldn't keep the house in a fit state for visitors. When gentlemen called they usually made a covert pass at him which he couldn't wait to tell me about.

'Signor Moreno pinched my bottom while you were playing the harpsichord!'

'I noticed. And *you* spilt coffee on him deliberately. He looked very offended when he stood up to leave. Have you forgotten we depend on him for business?'

Cherubino sulked for a few hours, then he went and picked me a bunch of mixed flowers from the parks and neighbouring gardens.

We made a list of men who had made passes at Cherubino. My maid kept jumping up and singing, '"*Madamina, il catalogo è questo; in Italia seicento e quaranta; in Allegmagna duecento e trentuna,* a hundred and two in Turkey, two hundred and two in France."'

'I've got a little list,' Cherubino continued, waving the paper scroll at me.

'You've got a little list,' I harmonised in falsetto.

'I'm more attractive than you, Marie-France,' Cherubino boasted.

'It's only because you're a maid,' I told him. 'They don't respect your feelings.'

'But I have the last laugh, don't I?' chimed Cherubino. 'I've got a little list, *son già mille e tre*, already one thousand and three.'

I never found out what Cherubino's real name was. He was born in Moravia apparently. I heard someone call him Oskar but he denied this was his own name.

'Why won't you tell me?' I pleaded.

'I like people thinking I'm Italian,' he replied.

'I tell you everything.'

'You've nothing to hide.'

Then he dressed himself as a nun — in a white tablecloth and a dark drape — just to spook me.

An officer knocked at the door with a warrant for Cherubino from the Emperor. It was his commission. They were sending him off to war. His name even appeared as Cherubino on the warrant. Imagine that. The Emperor was angry with my maid for his favourite mistress (like me) was in love with him. Cherubino was popular alright. The Emperor's mistress has worked out Cherubino was really a boy and the Emperor had heard about this too and he wasn't amused. They were both after him, but for different reasons. Cherubino was shaking all over. 'This is *real* Marie-France. Save me from those ag-ag-ag-aggressive men.'

'Save you? What about poor me?' I replied, thinking of myself left alone in Vienna.

I wanted to save him of course. I'd never seen him with chattering teeth before. He was usually the fearless one. I told the warrant officer who came banging on the door my singing maid was understudying *Orfeo* in the Burgtheater. Cherubino went and hid in the Ruprechtskirche belfry for five weeks until the Emperor forgave him, or maybe the Emperor's mistress forgot him. I never found out the real story.

Five long weeks. In the new city patience wasn't one of my seven virtues and five weeks was too long for me. Although I was under surveillance, every few days I prayed in the chapel and when no-one was looking I climbed the spiral staircase with food concealed in every crevice of my clothing.

When he heard footsteps Cherubino climbed inside the larger of the two bells — the enormous Angelus bell. It was burnished bronze. Probably medieval. Four Cherubinos could fit in there. What a throne for my maid. At the sound of my voice he leapt down from the clapper, clinging to the suspension ropes which would prevent him falling far if he lost his footing. His face was a sunflower, round and beaming. He wasn't wearing a dress (he was dressed like a man) but he was looking wonderful. Absence and all that ...

I had to take off most of my clothes to retrieve the parcels I'd been harbouring on my person. I placed the items of food on a makeshift shelf in the corner. The church sacristan has been supplying my fugitive with bread and buckets of water. Cherubino picked up everything on the shelf, considered it approvingly or disapprovingly, and put it down again. Did I bring him everything he wanted? What did I forget? I usually forgot something. 'At least I didn't forget to come,' I say crossly, stifling the sweetness I was feeling inside.

Cherubino sensed I was flooding and he responded by taking me in a headlock. I wriggled out of it. We had to be careful for there wasn't much room in the belltower, for a fight or for flight. There was a pile of cushions and covers in one corner and Cherubino nudged me towards them, forgetting about the food for the moment.

'You're a cauldron,' he claimed, hugging me, for with my swollen belly I was always much hotter than him. I wanted to lie down straightaway but first there was the struggle with his clothing. Cherubino wasn't resistant but his clothes were. I undressed him slowly for he had many layers on, and while I was doing this he stroked my hair.

We were making love when the bellringer started tugging ropes at the base of the tower, thirty feet below. Mass was about to be sung in the Ruprechstkirche, but this didn't deflect us from our task. We heard the sacristan's shout (it was his warning to us) and the creak of the ropes and the surging metal. The Angelus swung and clashed like the cymbals of Almighty God, splitting our ears in two.

I pressed my hands over Cherubino's ears and he held mine in the same way but nothing could prepare us for the might of the bell. It chimed through our bodies, breaking us into a thousand pieces of sound.

How long did the bell chime for?

We never timed it. Sometimes it was over in a minute and sometimes it rang for a long time, depending on the service of the day.

It was silent in the belfry, it had been silent for quite a while. Cherubino sighed and said his hearing was being damaged living beside bells. I sympathised, remembering what happened to my right eardrum in the convent. He said his singing may suffer as a result and this worried me too.

'It was so cold up here last night, Marie-France. I broke a chair into bits and lit a fire over there in a corner,' he told me.

'The light would be seen from the street.'

'I know. Risky, wasn't it?'

'Mmm,' I agree, thinking to myself it hardly mattered. I told him I'd received some good news. Signor Moreno called this morning to say the Emperor was about to pardon my cheeky maid. And there was also the matter of his commission.

'What's that?' Cherubino sat up, alert.

'No seal,' I informed him. 'The Emperor didn't stamp it with his seal.'

Cherubino looked relieved. He told me I was very clever to have noticed that.

'No seal, no deal,' I wise-cracked.

(I didn't tell him it was someone else who pointed this out to me.)

Cherubino realised he was going to be let off the hook. He stood up and wrapped the dress I arrived in around his bare haunches. Then he went over to the food waiting for him on the bench.

I rested for a while under the blankets, feeling calm and contented. Hearing singing in the street below, I pulled on Cherubino's white shirt and took a peek over the ledge of the belltower's arched window. The singers had moved on already. All I could see was the statue of Saint Ruprecht holding his tub of salt at the foot of the tower.

'Is the baby going to be born soon?' asked Cherubino, his cheeks full of Viennese sausage.

'It takes eight or nine months, you goose. Be a bit patient.'

Later I descended the spiral staircase alone, veiled from head to toe. At the entrance to the nave I came face to face with a nun carrying a candle. We looked at each other and I dropped her a curtsey, a sign of respect, a rush of guilt. She was a vision of myself from the past. She was also a measure of how far I had come. What did the nun think when she saw me, a woman heavy with child?

Now I knew things she could never aspire to know.

In the chapel I twisted rosary beads through my fingers, murmuring a catechism while the infant turned and fluttered in my womb. Oh merciful Mary. I never thought of myself as a sinner except when I went to mass. It continued to be my custom to go, despite my fallen state. (I'd heard news they were allowed to believe in God again in Avignon. But religious orders remained like vermin to the populace of France.)

After Cherubino was pardoned I quickly forgot he'd ever been under arrest and how distraught I'd been about it. I'd stopped holding on to things. Cherubino never held on to things, certainly not when it was pointless doing so. I copied his good traits and he copied mine. He was learning about responsibility and I was learning about freedom. Or maybe it was the other way around. I was learning responsibility, he was learning freedom. Whatever!

The weeks passed and we continued to repair old opera sets, creating some for new performances too. We lacked Walter's skill and expertise but we managed somehow. The workmen who delivered and collected these stage materials seemed to have forgotten Walter ever existed. My name appeared on the covers and packages. Shortly after this my name turned up on the household bills as well.

After a time I became too fat to move between the props in the restoration room. Cherubino and I could no longer squeeze into wardrobes together. After an hour's strenuous labour hemming the canopy of a four-poster bed for a forthcoming production of *Le Nozze di Figaro* I would fall asleep on the floor, then revive and be fresh for an outdoor stroll.

We went walking in the Belvedere Gardens with Cherubino in his *Figaro* clothes when the leaves from the city's forest of plane trees all decided to fall on the very same day. We were strolling through a veritable blizzard of wrinkled feathers and russet fans. Crunch, crunch, crunch. (But never forget: in the Viennese rain the leaves are mostly sodden underfoot.)

We found ourselves wading through brown-orange mounds, then swimming through leaves as they rose to our chins and kept falling. Cherubino disappeared into the soft damp surrounds as a fresh wave of tattered tree-linen wafted towards us. I wasn't the least concerned about him for the avalanche of leaves was as weightless as paper and children were squirming through layers like slippery eels.

Cherubino resurfaced in another section of the park. He had climbed one of the statues of the eight Muses and was shouting out my name, his arm wrapped around the Muse's waist. What blasphemy! He wasn't alone. People were climbing statues all over the gardens to gloat down on us leaf-clad strugglers wading through the soaking plumage.

A group of Viennese gentry, who'd been rehearsing an outdoor quadrille before the leaf storm, decided to continue their dance on the conveniently located squares of hedgerows, so that now they were dancing six feet off the ground. They simply climbed out of the mire of leaves and took up their positions on the manicured hedges above. Even the musicians had found places for themselves on top of bushes.

One of this party reached down for my hand and pulled me up onto a prickly hedgerow. He must have thought I was a member of their group. With my autumnal coat and Julius Caesar garland of leaves, the courtiers presumed I was somebody else. I found myself quickly drawn into their dance, taking their hands as we greeted each other and foot-skipped and turned, and when they called me Frieda I pretended to be her for there seemed little point in quibbling about it. They were convinced I must be she, so Frieda I became. (Lucky I know how to dance a quadrille.) I couldn't see Cherubino on the statue of the Muse any more. Where had he gone?

He'd climbed the royal pedestal and sat himself on the horse with the Emperor Joseph. This really was sacrilegious. Cherubino was sitting *in the emperor's lap*. He was waving at me through the paper-millage of floating leaves. I decided to take matters into my own hands. I called him over.

'Allegro vivace, Cherubino. Come and dance with us.'

He didn't respond. Cherubino could sing very well but he'd never learnt to dance for singers don't need to. As the quadrille is not the sort of dance you'd want to start with (and because the real Frieda had just surfaced through the mulch and was regarding me with disdain), I jumped down from my hedge, gulping on a mouthful of leaves, and swam through the foliage to join my maid on her high horse.

Though I refused to sit in the old emperor's lap I sat on the stallion's neck, face to face with my gold-flecked Cherubina, and consented to some smooching instead. By this time our faces and costumes and even our lips were plastered with wisps of tawny leaves.

'I hope you know who you're kissing,' Cherubino said to me, for with the camouflage of leaves it was impossible to tell.

'Everyone thinks I'm kissing a girl,' I said with much mirth.

'Just as well,' he replied, somewhat resentfully for I could still go cold on him if he dressed as a man. But it couldn't be helped. It was just one of those things. The past and the present aren't made for each other. They don't fold together like the wings of a bird.

I closed my eyes and the leaves were getting smaller now and turning green. All the trees in Vienna were losing their leaves and petals too were descending from above as waves of pleasure began to change into stabbing knives of pain.

It was happening to me this time. Not to Giselle or Violette or Our Lady milking a cow. It was happening to me. This was a blossoming belly I was wearing, wasn't it? This was meant to happen next year, next month or some other time. I wished it onto Frieda — she could have the baby for me and she could bring it up.

'I think I need a real horse to ride upon, Cherubino,' I said, recalling some advice of Violette's, once spoken on a swollen river.

'I think we'd better take cover in the leaves,' he replied.

For the next four hours I rolled through the mud and mulch, hardly aware of what I was doing or where I was going. I would lift my head up every five minutes to scream. I would bury it again when the pains went away. Sliding weightlessly through tunnels in the leaves I passed by many, coated in grime, who spoke consolingly to me. (I barely noticed them pass.) Someone with a spade kept throwing soil on my back and I told him not to stop.

Cherubino told me afterwards he was keeping close but I never thought of him. Like the dying I was somewhere else. I couldn't see, I couldn't hear, I could only feel. When I raised my head to cry, I opened my mouth wide and sound poured in from outside. It was the colour of bile. I drank my own scream then descended into the flooded vegetation which was warm and wet like a womb. I was moving more slowly as time went by.

I pushed the gardener with the spade away. I didn't need him any more. Shaking now, like I was back in the almshospital. This was familiar. Marie-Victoire, you served me well. With wisdom to guide me I knew my baby wasn't going to die. My hair hung over my eyes. I had lost Cherubino and would give birth in the Belvedere bog, alone.

Then I could feel something tugging on my body. My maid had attached a length of vine to a button on my petticoat. He was pulling himself towards me ...

I am down on my knees, pressing against him, kneading myself into earth when a sudden spray of water washes our bodies clean. A mighty push and Cherubino takes the head of our baby in his hands. The infant slips from me and I find myself gazing at a child already growing into someone larger than himself. He squalls, sits up, stands, then toddles away into the sea of faces, growing taller still as I watch him disappear. I have no time to worry about his fate for another infant is breaking between my legs. This time it is a girl and the same thing happens to her. She becomes a five year old in a matter of seconds and vanishes into the thicket of people-trees surrounding me. I lie back in agony and a third child is born. He quickly becomes a small boy, pees in my face, then runs naked into the bushes.

Cherubino's face expresses wonder as each miracle unfolds, and somehow I share his implicit faith. It must be so. How could I ever have expected it to be otherwise? If I'm tired I don't feel it. I could do this forever.

But a door in my body closes, never to open again.

I am wrapped in blankets and lifted into the arms of the waiting crowd. My daughter, recognisably the girl born ten minutes before, returns as a young woman, her face all aglow. She lies in the place I have been lying, her body big with child. She begins to labour and before I have time to catch my breath is giving birth to one infant after another just as I have done. Her children wander into the leaves, re-emerging as fully grown and costumed adults. Impossible but true. My grandchildren!

Now my daughter is lifted in blankets and I am shaken free of mine like breadcrumbs. My body has dispersed into fragments of light, into ashes, my spirit thickening into impermeable matter as though an exchange has been made between this world and the next.

'Cherubino, Cherubino, Cherubino,' I cry out. We are pressed against each other so forcefully I can only gasp. Is this joy or suffocation? I see our future generations, a long line of descendants with musical gifts and sonorous voices.

Furthest away is Ilka, wife of Hungarian Háry and daughter of Arkel, who is the son of Lulu, who is the daughter of Mathis, who is the son of Jitka, who is the daughter of Werther, who is the son of Rosa, who is the daughter of Rodrigo, who is the son of Mireille, who is the daughter of Simon the beggar student, who is the son of Erda.

Stars of the night sky that blink open and shed light. Jewelled voices of the future stage.

Each birth contains all seasons, songs and funeral pyres.

I will never be quite myself, again.

In Vienna the trees are bare and no leaves fall, but the rain is pelting down. The infant in my arms is a normal newborn size. Umbrellas appear. A kindly gentlewoman wipes my body clean and helps me change into dry clothing. Another is swaddling the baby tightly before returning him to me. The palace officials and residents have been alerted. They arrive bearing gifts, wanting to assist.

I am carried to a small tent-shaped pavilion, recently swept clear of leaves. The rain stops for it's growing dark, but there is a persistent dripping from the roof and nearby branches. Iron lamps are lit in the gardens. Someone gives Cherubino a lantern to hold and we are left in peace, just the three of us and the light glowing in Cherubino's hands.

I'm lying down exhausted and my vision is blurry. In the future I would always remember the sense I had of the light emanating directly from Cherubino's body. The flame had a source somewhere within him. The light flowed out of the lantern like a genie out of a bottle and the vessel itself was no longer visible. A butter-coloured cloud rested on Cherubino's chest like a pillow.

The baby stirs and snuffles in my arms. My little boy. *Our* child. So I sit up awkwardly, finding my body sore in many places, and offer the infant to Cherubino. He accepts and I take the lantern in exchange. Looking through the glass I see the flickering candle of my spirit and the pulse of my heart. I turn away and my eyes meet the gentle radiance of the moon, low in the sky tonight, hazy through clouds. I lift the lantern up, resting it over father and son, as if to warm them. Beneath the light Cherubino's hair turns a strange coppery colour, like a crown of coins. The baby's face is pink and mauve. Only a small triangle is exposed to the night air — his flat nose, closed eyes and the perfect pin-tuck of his mouth.

'You wanted a girl,' Cherubino fondly accuses.

'That's because girls usually live longer and have sweeter temperaments.'

'This one looks healthy,' Cherubino says confidently.

'Yes, he does.'

I can't believe I've just had a baby. I keep telling myself I survived, I survived. In my head I'm saying, 'I'm a mother, I'm a mother,' but it has yet to sink in. I'd rather hold the lantern than our child, such is my state of shock. I'm fraying at the edges but the light is stronger than any fear and confusion. It wraps a golden thread around the three of us, it binds us together and makes us one.

Author's Notes

Chapter One: The 'brigands' are described in Thomas Carlyle's *The French Revolution*, p108, as 'troops of ragged Lackalls' enlisted by both democrats and aristocrats to support their respective causes. Chapman & Hall Ltd, London, 1906 (first published 1836).

Chapter Two: The descriptions of Giselle's clothes and of the women of Provence during the late eighteenth century are taken from Michel Biehn's *Colors of Provence*, Flammarion, Paris, 1996.

Chapter Three: The quote from Teresa of Avila is taken from *The Complete Works of St Teresa of Jesus, Volume 1, The Life*, Sheed & Ward, London, 1946.

Chapter Four: The quote from Bernard of Clairvaux is taken from Julia Kristeva's *Tales of Love*, Columbia, New York, 1987. Her discussion of the saint's metaphysical ideas in Chapter Four of *Tales of Love* was also influential in the creation of my Chapter Four, 'The Dance Academy of Avignon'.

Chapter Seven: The sentence beginning, 'Crack, crack, crack, went the coach driver with his whip ...' bears the influence of a similar description in Laurence Sterne's *The Life & Opinions of Tristram Shandy*, Penguin, London, 1967 (first published 1759-67).